For Robby Sukhdeo and all
those who give themselves
to communities – S.B.

For Michael and
Maggie Cohen – N.S.

Dear Reader,

This is a story long in the telling,
planted into childhood,
finding form and wings in words.
When shadows fall you stand beside, so says Omid.
His message I too stand by.

This is a story that has your back.
It stands by you –
who walk this tender earth –
seeking light.

This is a story-tree of survival
with world-wandering roots,
a strong trunk,
wide reaching, sustaining branches
for all to shelter under,
in family, friendship, community, love.

This story is in your hands
to have and to hold.
In it you will find the passing of a pen
and charcoal to make art from scorched earth.
Take it up and feel its force,
for now is your time to fly.

Sita Brahmachari

LiTTLE TiGER
LONDON

When Shadows Fall contains content some readers may find triggering as it explores trauma, including loss of a child, racism, addiction, depression, suicide attempt and gang violence.

STRIPES PUBLISHING LIMITED

An imprint of the Little Tiger Group
1 Coda Studios, 189 Munster Road,
London SW6 6AW

Imported into the EEA by Penguin Random House Ireland,
Morrison Chambers, 32 Nassau Street, Dublin D02 YH68

www.littletiger.co.uk

First published in Great Britain by Stripes Publishing Limited in 2021
Text copyright © Sita Brahmachari, 2021
Art copyright © Natalie Sirett, 2021

HB ISBN: 978-1-78895-316-0
PB ISBN: 978-1-78895-436-5

The Forest Stewardship Council® (FSC®) is a global, not-for-profit organization dedicated to the promotion of responsible forest management worldwide. FSC defines standards based on agreed principles for responsible forest stewardship that are supported by environmental, social, and economic stakeholders. To learn more, visit www.fsc.org

2 4 6 8 10 9 7 5 3 1

WHEN SHADOWS FALL

SITA BRAHMACHARI

ILLUSTRATED BY NATALIE SIRETT

Prologue

I'll tell you what this is not going to be. It won't be a sob story. It won't be a gut-wrenching tragedy, though there is that, for definite. It's not one of those stories where you watch me fall and fall and fall, though I do.

What can I say? I'm here today, aren't I?

I suppose my point in writing this is so that somehow, in all the mess that was made, I can put what happened to me, to us, to some use. See how I don't say the mess *I* made or *we* or *they* made or even *he* or *she* or *they* made. I say *was* made. Though nothing felt passive about it.

Who the hell am I talking to? Not the ravens. They've flown this world, though I do keep looking for Bow. Got to let her go.

I've written this for me.

Kai.

I.

It's summer now, though there was a time that felt like eternal winter. If you ever get sucked into Shadowlands remember: no matter how bleak, seasons change.

So here I am, sitting on our Green Hill, writing this…

There is a green hill far away without a city wall.

Strange how you think you're doing the writing then lines from songs bombard your mind and write into you.

There is a green hill,
far away,
without a city wall.

I sang this hymn once with Dad at Christmas, standing outside St Paul's Cathedral, listening to the choir practising. Dad was banging on about bringing me back there to sing one day. What was it he said? "Everyone has the right to raise their voice and hear it echoing round a place as awesome as St Paul's."

It still gives me shivers to hear our Green Hill song. I suppose it's because it's the first tune he played on his sax when I came back. It always gets me, the way it builds so predictably then creeps up on you and steals your heart with the minor keys… Cuts me up every time.

Here's what I wish I could have told myself when I was wading through crap. You know those interviews where people say what they would have said to their teenage selves? I can't believe I still am one. An oversized teenager staying on for another year at sixth form while my mates all fly away. Anyway, *get over yourself, Kai,* as Orla says. Get on with it.

Well, if I could speak to me, how I was then, I'd tell myself to remember this green hill was always waiting for us. To look down on the past and see ourselves in the pools of light, shining like raven wings after rain.

That doesn't even sound like me! Why is it so hard to read back your own words? Like stripping stark bollock naked and walking up the street, your whole self out there, exposed, even though I'm the only one reading it, for now anyway. I leaf through the pages where I attempted to write some kind of ending for what happened – torn or scrubbed out because everything I wrote just felt so lame… Maybe that's what writing this has been all about – starting at the end with a lot of help from my friends, finding my way back, not to normal … but back.

On our balcony behind me Dad's playing his sax again.

Something he's composing. My friends are celebrating getting their A levels and I'm here on our Greenlands hill by Sula's tree, waiting for them. How long can it take to pick up a few results? The answer comes back and slaps me in the face… In my case, no matter how fast I've tried to catch up, another year.

Nothing's what it looks like from the outside, is it? I've clocked this scene before; it's an old story. I suppose anywhere in the world it looks the same. Brothers and sisters at the point of breaking out. From where I'm sitting now it's all about an eighteen-year-old boy and his mates, setting out to leave the bit of turf they've made their own and fly in different directions.

Nothing mythical about this moment. But till now, if you'd told me I'd *ever* have it in my sights to even be sitting here, reading over my story, waiting for my mates and thinking this time next year I'll be down there, walking through the high railings of Ravenscroft with my own results, I would have said, "You're dreaming!"

They're taking ages.

I run my hands over the soft surface of my notebook that I've crammed full of our takes on what went on, pictures and words, nothing spared. All the shit we went through. This notebook, Orla's early birthday present to me… Her voice jogs me back. I could pick her tone out in any crowd.

Here she comes, leading the way, Om and Zak trailing

behind her, past the flattened earth where our Bothy used to be, past the old metal railings that lead out of Ravenscroft, the place they're leaving now forever.

Orla... Or-laaaaaaa, Or-leeeeeee... I always want to sing her name like the first two notes of a love song. Old habits.

Zak, my first best mate who took all I threw at him and refused to give up on me.

And by their side walks Om. My newest friend and oldest soul brother. It feels like I've known him forever, like we knew each other in another life or something.

Watching them make their way up the Green Hill of our growing, I think I never really understood what Om tried to explain, why his family died defending the ancient buildings of Aleppo instead of running for their lives. But, when I think about how we're still battling to hold on to this triangle of Greenlands wood and our little bit of Rec, maybe I do start to get it. Saving a place isn't just about the land – it's about saving us too, our memories of home... I have to stop feeling sorry for myself and stay and fight for our Greenlands, for all of us. Like Om's family guarded their home. What's the big deal? I'm safe. No bombs are raining down on *my* head.

Get over yourself, Kai... Orla's right. It's time I do. Dig deep and keep fighting. This is something worth guarding.

"We did good." My friends' voices bring me back as

they tumble down beside me. They must have rehearsed this moment as I knew they would. Not to turn results day into a big deal.

Zak hands me an envelope. "Mum said to give this to you."

"What is it, a consolation prize?" I snap but Orla shoves me in the back.

"Didn't tell me what it was, just said make sure you get it." Zak shrugs.

"Thanks." Maybe one day we'll shrug off all the awkwardness between us. I put the envelope in my pocket.

Om's portfolio is tucked under his arm and he thrusts it at me. "Here! I packed away my exhibition. This is for you."

I shake my head. "No, Om, man. It's too much. I can't take this."

But he grabs my face and holds it in his hands, like his aunt does to him. "No argument. It is my gift."

Orla lets out a sob behind him. "We said to keep it light, Om!"

I want to say something but there's too much and too many words between us. I don't know what comes over me but I spring on Zak and wrestle him to the ground like we haven't done since we were kids.

Just sparring, at least I can't *feel* any anger left in us as we roll down our Green Hill.

We're sprawled out on the grass now, cloud surfing like we used to. Om takes his phone from his pocket, insisting on a group selfie. He's obsessed. Like he thinks he'll lose everything if it's not recorded. I get that. He almost did.

"You're sure about giving me all this art, Om? If you change your mind…"

"I am done with this." He waves it away as if it's nothing. "Zak, Orla… Get in the picture! Close, closer," he orders.

We're all squeezed together, just about fitting in the frame. Here we are, caught in time forever. Me, Orla, Om and Zak gathered round Sula's tree. In this moment it's all laughter, though if you do look close and closer through the shafts of light, you might just make out the rainbow spirits of ink-black wings.

Om's not happy with the shot and we all know he won't let us go till he is.

Finally.

"This is honest shot! Looking for the future," Om announces, showing us ourselves peering out of the photo, squinting into the sunshine, our bodies casting long shadows…

Just then Orla's mum and Om's aunt call from their balconies, eager to celebrate their results.

And trailing off, one by one, they leave me to it.

I pick up the notebook, turning to the beginning again, but realize something's missing... A dedication. Who knows when or if the wounds will heal enough to let my mates read this whole thing. Truth is I'm struggling myself to get through, but if they do ever read it the least I can do is write them a dedication. If I can just find words strong enough, loyal enough, kind enough, brave enough to hold what my mates have done for me. I turn the pages and find the place I left off reading.

See ourselves in the pools of light, shining like raven wings after rain...

That is how it feels turning way, way back to when we were kids. Like walking in pools of light.

Act 1

Voice Unbroken

Kai

When I was a kid
Dad was always song-weaving,
singing of rainbows and what's at the end of them.
I didn't know if it was fairy tale, myth ... or whatever.
That was back when I thought my parents could save me,
fly me to golden places,
hold me,
never let me fall.

In myth time you think they know what they're doing.
Then comes an age
when you discover that they can fall too,
so you have to work out new rules.
Maybe you can and maybe you can't
or
maybe you break them instead.

Then you're in the eye of the storm,
flying inside myth
where anything can happen
and this time there's no turning back,

you're in it before you know it.
No one warns you that the border's spun
fine as a spider's web.

I'm sorry, friends.
Before you knew it you got caught up with me
but this is the web we've woven together.
It's tangled, torn, tortured even,
and I could never have told it
alone,
shouldn't.
And even though I need to know what you've written,
what sense you've made of everything that happened,
I'm also dreading it.
If this were music
it would be more Dad's wild jazz improv
than the tunes I know
where I can picture where my voice will land
in clean, clear notes like
'Somewhere Over the Rainbow'.

Time to cut through
if I'm ever going to do what I've told myself I will
and help other kids clinging on to the high wire
to work themselves out,

pick themselves up.
or better still
catch them before they're pushed,
jump,
fall...
Then I always knew this was the only way through.
To spin this together.

But now my part's done
there's this weird emptiness that the writing
and dreaming of Orla used to fill
and fear's creeping in.
If only I could be
moving on like everyone else.

Is this another of what Dad calls "forging moments"?
How many do people have of these
earthquakes, storms, hurricanes
in their lifetime?
How many can you take?

I think what I'm chatting about
is the mammoth moments of transformation,
metamorphosis, whatever...

It's been all right writing this,
knowing my mates would help piece together what I can't,
but when they've flown
I'm going to have plenty more times like this,
sitting here on my own.
Then what?
I've done all the thinking about who was here
with me,
for me.
Not the ones who had to be
or should have been like family,
I mean the people I chose
or who chose me.
Whichever way,
for better or worse,
it's written.

Notebook in hand,
sitting on this Green Hill,
waiting for my mates to fill in the voids.

Maybe when I've read what they each have to say
I'll find a way to cut and paste it.
To make a proper book for myself.
Strange sort of tale that would be,

written by humans and ravens,
who picked and pecked up the pieces whenever I lost my way.
Because that's what friends do.
Friends ... more than
friends,
who have your back
no matter how much pain you're in
or how much pain you've put them through,
who hold you so you don't fall,
isn't that true?

When I couldn't make any sense of where I was
or even who I was
they stepped in.

They lived through the times when my words slipped away.

Orla
    Zak
        Om
           Rain
              Bow

all have skin,
or feathers,
in the game.

This was never only my story to tell.
That's the thing
that always goes against the lie
of the I – the self,
of me and my.

I have this strange feeling of lifting out of myself ... as if I'm telling someone else's story. I gaze up through the canopy of Greenlands trees, still searching for my ravens. Maybe that's the way to read this... Imagine I'm the one who's flying above, looking down on who we were.

The earliest memories are the easiest.

Deep sigh.
Fly, Kai,
fly.
Fly back...

To a kaleidoscope of screeching, swirling dots careering round the playground. No... I haven't flown back far enough.

How old am I? Three or four maybe? It's the summer before I start school. I have my own cutters, small and blunt. Dad's got me kitted out in bright yellow overalls, thick garden gloves, wellington boots and swimming goggles. He wears overalls too, though his are navy blue. I like that we're the same. Young, handsome, unlined, long-locked Dad is right here ahead of me, brandishing his sharp cutters in the air. My invincible warrior dad.

"We are men armoured against the thorns! Greenlands Guardians." I close my eyes against the pain of Dad's laughter. His deep, strong laughter, low and sure. My little boy voice sweet, unbroken, comes to me sharp and clear.

This is the feeling I have. That my dad is strong enough to shake the earth we're standing on.

At this moment in time I love my dad so hard that it hurts. It is before the moment the world comes rushing in. Before school and way, way, way before Sula's tree was planted. This is the summer of stories and songs, of cutting new paths further every day into the steep, brambled path that leads down the Green Hill from our flat.

This is the summer that Mum's taking her exams to be a nurse and it's just me and Dad, wild and happy, randomly bursting into song and building our den.

Ah! And they are there too, the ravens, nameless then.

Cawing through my mind.

**I'm missing Bow so much right now.
Stay present, Kai.**

I am afraid of the ink-winged birds as they settle around us, but Dad isn't. "Good afternoon!" he jokes. "D'you think they look a bit like me in my doorman suit?"

I shake my head, backing away. I am cautious of these raucous creatures, won't stray too near them, and I'm not the only one. Mum always flaps her hands at them like she's frightened, wants them gone. No matter how many times Dad laughs and says they're harmless, I run away, leaping into his arms to safety. And every time he sings the same silly song.

Don't fear the ravens, Kai.
Look to the shine in their eye.
See how the light glints on their feathers,
painting rainbows on ebony wings.
Look to the shine in their eye,
Kai.
Look to the shine in their eye.

Each day Dad tells me tales of the ravens and slowly

my fears ebb away. "This piece of woodland wilderness we're clearing belongs as much to these ravens as to us, my Kai!"

Huddled in our den of sticks Dad spins stories of how ravens have nested here since the beginning of time. "If we're going to share this wilderness, if you're to one day walk through the high gates of Ravenscroft 'Big' School, then you've got to learn to trust the ravens!"

I block my ears. I don't like it when he says things like this. If Mum hears she tells him not to fill my head with nonsense. "Don't take any notice, Kai. By the time you go there, you'll be all grown and the gates won't seem so high." Mum reassures me but woven in Dad's stories I always hear his sighs. I'm not supposed to know but I heard him say to Mum once how he hated school so much he used to run away.

I am happy, maybe at my happiest, building dens in Greenlands, learning to trust the ravens. Dad teaches me the names and calls of sweet songbirds as we thrash our way through brambles. His favourite is the thrush. Mine's between that and the robin that's brave enough to hop within touching distance of us. Dad stops, places his finger to his lips and we hold our breath, listening to its song and playing statues, seeing who can go the longest without moving.

Just us and the birds in the world.

High above the den the mottled-bellied thrush sings her song and we watch the mother busying herself. Dad says there's bound to be a nest. "Shh – we mustn't disturb her whatever we do because –" and he leans into me, close like he's going to share the most important secret in the world – "their nests are little low heavens… Their eggs the most perfect shade of blue anyone could ever paint."

He makes us tiptoe up the steep hill and under my breath I whisper,

"Little low heavens,

little low heavens,

little low heavens."

I was too young to think this then, but if I could have put into words what I felt that day it would have been that maybe we're song thrushes too! Living in our Greenlands nest, our little low heaven.

I'm straining my neck to the ground-floor balcony where Mum stands waving as we climb the final stretch of steep hill.

"But look yonder … Juliet my love!"

"Don't talk funny again, Dad! Why do you call Mum Juliet when her name's Janice?"

But Dad just ruffles my hair. "I hope you'll know one day!" he answers, laughing.

"Look at the state of you two!" As we get closer I see Mum's eyes are bloodshot tired. Dad throws his arms out wide, reaching up towards her. I copy him and it makes Mum giggle. I wish our balcony could go straight out on to Greenlands, instead of the lock-ups getting in the way. Then it really would feel like ours.

"Why can't we have steps from our wood to our balcony?" I ask and Dad chuckles, looking up at Mum, the shine in his eye sparking with happiness.

"Now there's an idea for a lyric – a stairway to our little low heaven!" I hear him whisper as we walk round the block through the cold metal clanking door.

"Juliet… Wherefore—"

Mum opens our door, shaking her head, but she's not really cross with us. "You idiot, Dex! Get in!"

Dad gathers Mum in his arms and swirls her around till she begs him to put her down.

"Look what we did, Mum!" I say, running out to the balcony.

From here you can see our progress. We stand together ,just the three of us, watching the sun setting over the path we're cutting through the brambles. The path through the triangle of woodland that Dad says is no-man's land, so why not claim it as ours.

Mum wipes a smear of blackberry juice from my cheek.

"What on earth have you two been up to?"

"Taming our very own Greenlands garden!" Dad announces.

"You're a dreamer, Dexter King."

"Yep! That's why you love me!"

Dad puts some music on and they hold each other, Mum and Dad, swaying to a rhythm I can't hear. But when I stand on Dad's feet, clinging to his legs, and close my eyes I can feel it playing through them.

Love.

"You better go and get yourself cleaned up!" Mum pulls away from Dad, bends down and plants a kiss on my muddy forehead.

Dad runs the bath and plays his bubble-blowing trick, soaping his hands till they're covered, dipping them in water and prising his thumb and fingers apart "ever-so-slowly" until a great shiny orb forms. When he's sure it won't break he gives me the nod. Lips pursed, eyes saucer-wide at the miracle giant bubble, I "ever-so-gently" blow it through his hands.

"Make a wish, Kai!" he whispers.

Then we eat together on the balcony. Dad goes inside and dresses in his black work suit that he hates wearing more than anything. But he says it could be worse. At least he gets to stand at the Jazz Café door and listen to music he loves, "when it's not drowned out by the noise of the street".

I don't see why he isn't one of the acts inside because my dad's the best musician in the whole wide world. I tell him what I think and he looks like he could cry but instead ruffles my hair and says, "Thanks, Kai. You're the best son in the whole wide world."

He always deep-sighs before he leaves. "Once more into the urban jungle!" he jokes but the shine has gone from his eyes and mine too. Because wishing that Dad would never have to work through the night, that he could sometimes read me into dreaming, never comes true. The magic of the day always ends, the bubble bursts, when he sets out.

First day of school. Do I remember it? I *think* I do. But maybe this is just lots of different pictures crashing against each other. Collage-memory connecting. Synapses finally lighting up. What does it matter? It *feels* like the first day of school, so let's say it is. Who's arguing? Maybe one day if I let Zak read this he'll have another take on it.

I see myself hanging back against the climbing frame, waving to Dad who's carrying the ball we dribbled into school together.

Ha! If I could I would run up to myself and give me a hug.

I raise my head and come face-to-face with Zak, beaming his missing-teeth grin.

He was there for me on day one and he's still here now, although half the time we haven't got a clue what to say to each other.

Out of nowhere a ball lands at my feet. "Want to play?" Zak asks. I bite my lip, tears stinging my eyes as I watch Dad cross the Rec. Ravens fly with him – I wish they wouldn't. "Go on! Kick it!" Zak says.

I shake my head but Zak comes over to me where I cling to the railings.

In no time we're cartwheeling, stretching our arms and flying like ravens. I teach Zak Dad's song and we career around, arm-wings soaring, chanting together.

Don't fear the ravens, Kai.
Look to the shine in their eye.

On the way home Dad brings my football and we dribble it across the playing fields of our Rec. I tell him about my new best friend.

"If I have a brother I think he'll look a bit like Zak," I tell Dad.

He winks at me and says, "You never know, son. Maybe you will have a brother or sister one day."

I screw up my nose. "I only want a brother!"

Dad sighs and says, "Babies don't come to order." Then he whacks the ball off the football pitch and far across the Rec so I sprint after it and wait on the Greenlands path for him. I'm doubled over while I catch my breath. When Dad reaches me he's out of breath too and he crouches down and points into the brambles that mark the beginning of Greenlands wood. "I've been thinking maybe one day we could cut through from here all the way home," he pants.

"Why?" I ask. Even standing on my tiptoes, I can't see Greenlands tower over the top of our Green Hill on the other side of our wild wood. I like that anyone walking on this Rec wouldn't know our den's in there.

"To make a short cut down to the Rec, instead of having to walk the long way round on the path to Greenlands.

How about you ask Zak over, see if he wants to help us with our clearing?"

Dad picks up a long stick and pushes it through the thicket till I can hear it tapping on the metal railings that back on to Ravenscroft Secondary School, where me and Zak will go one day. But as he thrashes around with his stick, beating through, my gut tangles ... like opening up our path really wouldn't be a good idea. Greenlands is our secret kingdom, mine and Dad's, and, even though Mum's always telling Dad off for wasting so much time down here with me, I don't want us ever to be finished with clearing it.

Back home Mum opens her arms and I run at her, telling her about my new friend Zak, and she smiles and says how she still remembers her first school friend. I wait for her to tell me more but she hurries me through to jump into the bath. She's walking round our flat, picking up washing and cleaning the kitchen, and Dad's just about to blow a mammoth wishing bubble when Mum drops in a clean towel and says she needs to borrow Dad for a "little chat". I can hear their bickering through the door.

I wonder why Dad never calls Mum Juliet any more. Her voice is not chatty but angry and she's saying how she's working hard and studying for her nursing exams and how Dad needs to find more work and how she can't make ends meet (I don't know what that means). Now she's saying she can't do it on her own any more. It all comes out in a rush.

But she's not on her own. I don't understand. She's always telling off Dad for not looking for more work, not just his nightshift. She's not shouting but her words punch at the air.

Then I hear Dad say, "I told you I'd put my name forward for football coach for after school!"

"Is it paid though? We need the money, Dex! I'm wearing myself out here! Sign up for it anyway. It might lead to something. Better than idling your time away in that wilderness every day, filling Kai with nonsense stories about ravens."

"They're not nonsense stories," I want to scream at Mum. I don't know what "idling" means but it doesn't sound good. I slide under the water so I don't have to listen to the "discussion". That's what they call it, but it's arguing really and I'm trying to work out how I'm going to break the news that Zak's dad has already started coaching us.

When Dad comes back through I refuse to get out of the bath till he blows a proper wishing bubble. I scrunch my eyes tight and wish my usual wish – that he starts to call Mum Juliet again.

I let it out that Zak's dad's our coach and he just shrugs,

wraps me in the towel and flies me out of the bath on to the floor. But I can see he wishes he could be coach as much as I do.

"But Dad? It's not fair. I wished for you. Did you tell them you used to be professional?"

"That was a lifetime ago, son! They can't all come true, your wishes!"

Seems like none of them do. Not for me, not for Dad either.

Tonight, just before Dad sets out to work, he plays some music that's too sad to dance to so I make him change it. Grabbing Mum's hand and his, I pull them close together, standing on their feet so they have to stay close or they split me. We sway together, my arms wrapped round them both. Even though the music's happy now, I can still feel sad music beating through them.

I haven't talked aloud to Bow since I returned. I'm trying not go back to that but it's strange what writing does to you. It's sort of released this thing in me. I imagine I'm talking to Sula as if she and not the tree were beside me... Sometimes I catch myself muttering the words as I'm writing them down, as if she really is here, listening. Is there any harm in picturing that?

I had some faith in wishing on bubbles for a while because Dad got to step in as coach when Zak's dad was pushed for time ... but it still didn't make Mum happy because no one paid him and it led to an even more explosive argument. I do remember her saying one thing, because it's bitten into me so many times over the years. The truth does bite. "If you don't value yourself, Dexter, no one will ever take you seriously."

Is that when I first noticed Dad was losing the shine in his eye?

So while I couldn't put any of this into words back then, I sort of sensed it, knew things were sliding, but kicked it to the back of my mind because whatever worries I had, as soon as Dad was coaching us at footie, they were gone.

"What does 'value yourself' mean?" I ask Dad on the way to footie.

"How much you're worth," Dad mumbles, dribbling the ball to me.

"But you're worth my dad!" I protest.

"Seems that's not enough, Kai."

"Why?" I pass it back.

"Forget I said that." He picks up the ball and breaks into a jog. "Come on, son! Let's win this game!"

Kai, Kai, pass.

Kai, cross, Kai!

Got it!

Fly with the ball.

I'm the sprinter,

"the dancer" Dad calls me.

He's taught me all his tricks.

How to balance
a spinning ball on my
toe,

how to twist mid-air,

footie pirouette.

Me and Zak, because we're always together, can read each other's thoughts from far off.

I judge the placing,

read the twist of his shoulder,

> tilt of his head
>
> giving me the nod
>
> of where to plant the ball
>
> at his feet,
>
> weaving in and out until he scores
>
> and Dad blows the whistle.
>
> Triumphant.
>
> "Poetry in motion, you two!" he shouts, scooping us both
> into his arms.

After the match Zak's mum and dad come over to shake hands
with him. Zak's dad says, "The team's come on so much!
You're a great coach! Thought of doing it professionally?"

"He is professional!" I butt in.

"Almost was!" Dad laughs, ruffling my hair. "I did play for
a bit but got an injury," he explains like he's embarrassed.
"It's just for fun these days!" Dad smiles, chipping at the
churned-up ground, but I can see that he's flushed with
pride and I am too.

My dad is worth a lot.
My dad is a good coach.
My dad is worth a lot.
My dad is a great musician.
My dad is worth a lot.

Sometimes I wish Zak didn't live on the other side of the Rec. I've been to his house loads of times but he's never been to mine. "Can Zak come back to ours?" I beg, both of us caked in mud.

On our way home I tell Dad that all the houses on Zak's road have gardens with enough space for football nets. Suddenly Dad sets off at a sprint so we have to run to catch up with him. For some reason he's decided that today's the day to open up our secret short cut. "We don't have a garden but we have got this – our very own wilderness wood. You're filthed up anyway, boys – come this way!"

We're on hands and knees, following the railings of Ravenscroft School. We're struggling a bit so Dad hunts for long sticks and passes us one each to beat our way through.

"Your dad's brilliant!" Zak's eyes flash with excitement as we swish, bash and crawl our way through the undergrowth. I nod, fit to burst with pride. I lead the way now, knowing that soon our cutting through will open up to the path that leads to Greenlands.

We scramble up the bank we've cleared. I show Zak our den as we slip and slide on watery clay. At the top of the Green Hill we catch our breath, looking back to where we've come from.

We were here. Our clay-encrusted feet and hands planted on this ground. Right where I wrote this, right here where I sit now, reading it through beside Sula's tree, though nothing of this was planted then. I lay my book down because the tears are dripping on to the page, smudging the words. These memories are scored deep into me. It's like now I'm scratching at old scars, picking at hard-crusted scabs, making myself bleed. A bit of me wants to rip everything up.

A shaft of sunlight falls on Sula's tree as if she, who never spoke a word, is speaking now, encouraging me to carry on writing. "Do this for me."

Take Dad's advice... Keep in the present of the past if you're going to go there, I coach myself. *He's right! He should know, I suppose. It makes it possible to face it all.*

"You're so lucky. Is this really all your wilderness wood?" Zak sighs, wide-eyed as we sit together, me, Dad and Zak. The trees are bare above us. A pair of ravens perch in the spindly branches, squawking insistently, making sure we don't forget it's their land too.

I look to Dad for an answer because I know it's not exactly true that it's all ours. Not like Zak's garden is his. "Yep! All ours. We're its guardians." Dad nods, not meeting Zak's eyes, looking off into the distance through the trees.

Mum calls from the balcony for us to hurry up and get in the bath before we catch our deaths.

When we're inside I start a running commentary of the match. She says well done, but I can tell she's more interested that I've got a friend with me, and I think, from the nod she gives to Dad, that she's happy he invited Zak. She's waiting at the door with bin bags, makes us strip off our kit and marches us through to a steaming hot bath.

This is the day I teach Zak how to make the best giant wishing bubbles and seven year old could ever blow. I couldn't believe no one had taught him. "My dad's a champion bubble blower," I boast.

Soap, soap, soap.
Then make a heart with your thumbs and first finger of
both hands.
Slowly, slowly open the heart.
Blow gently, letting the shape grow however it wants,
                              until it floats free…

We watch like it's a race between our wishing bubbles. Zak's get caught on the mirror edge and bursts but mine floats out of the door and we spring from the bath, trailing froth and murky water, chasing it to my room and out through the open windows. We stand on my balcony, shivering, watching my giant bubble drift down the steep mound that leads to Greenlands…

Mum comes running out, fretting about the soaking carpet and us catching a cold. "What will Zak's parents think of us?"

Mum's always worrying about what people think of us but Dad doesn't care. We're not cold at all, still steaming from the bath. She throws towels over us as we watch my giant bubble drift away.

"You can share my wish!" I tell Zak.

"OK!" He nod, and Mum places a hand on both our shoulders.

"Never too old for wishing!" she whispers with her eyes scrunched closed like she's making one too.

I know what she's wishing for because I hear Mum and Dad whispering about it all the time. As well as the wish for Dad to be worth more, and for her not to have to work so hard all the time, she wants a baby brother or sister for me. I wish she wouldn't say she wants it for me. I don't care that much, as long as they stop arguing.

The way Mum's knuckles turn white from holding on to the balcony railings while she's wishing makes me feel sad and I reach for her hand. I think Mum's been making the same wish for a long time so, instead of my usual wish for Dad not to have to go to work at night, I wish for a baby too.

I hear the metal door to the outside slam. With our free hands we wave to Dad as he heads out into the dark.

"Your dad looks smart in his work suit!" Zak says.

Under the lamplight Dad pulls a face and starts to do his funny raven dance, flapping the ends of his black jacket to make me laugh like he always does but suddenly it's not OK. I wish he wouldn't play the fool with Zak here.

Zak creases up and I make like it's funny too, but I've seen the look on Mum's face and it makes me want to cry because she knows as much as I do how Dad hates wearing his raven suit.

When Zak's gone and Mum comes to say goodnight I tell her, "It's OK, Mum. If another baby doesn't come. Zak can be my brother."

But as soon as I say it I wish I'd kept my mouth shut because now she has tears in her eyes and I think it's me who made her cry.

Hard to pinpoint the day when I started to feel there were things that were better left unsaid, best to be quiet... It seems young to have decided that, but I think it was around then that I began folding in on myself. Orla called it: writing this while she and Zak are away at their festival or working at their summer camp, whatever, has got me thinking deep about how I was back then, more than I've ever done before.

I remember how I felt with an acid ache inside like hunger.

And just when I started to feel the bubbles bursting who should appear in my life but Orla.

A light breeze loosens a cluster of dry leaves and I follow their tumbling golden path, illuminated by the sunshine, coming to settle on the flat earth that was once our den. The chasing leaves turn my memory back to golden times when I was ten years old. I didn't know it yet, but this was going to be one of those mammoth days.

Dad doesn't come down to our wood so much any more but he says I'm allowed to stray as far as our den on my own … as long as he can still see me from the balcony. He says he has to practise his sax and I ask him if that's because they're going to let him inside the Jazz Café, not stand at the door in his suit.

"In my dreams!" He sighs, no shine in his eye. "Don't worry about it, Kai… You and your mum are the only audience I need."

I turn and wave to him. From down here I can still hear him play. At this distance it sounds like the saddest cry in all the world. Why can't he and Mum play happy music?

In our den I turn over a stone and woodlice scurry away. I listen to Dad and try to work out what's happening. I take a stick and dig a hole and I think it's like he's hunting for something buried so deep in the earth that it can only be brought to the surface by music.

I'm smoothing the mud back over the hole I've made as Dad's playing comes to an end. I'm just wondering if he'll come down now he's finished, when I hear voices. A girl and a woman. No one ever comes here except me and Dad and, if he's with me, Zak. I freeze but I want to run out and shout at them to go away… This Greenlands wilderness is ours.

"It's not really a garden, Mum," the girl says, who from what I can see is about my age.

Were those the first words I heard you say? I think they were... Hard to think of a time when your voice did not fill my mind.

"How about I fix up your swing permanently right here over this tree?" The woman peers back over to our block. "I'll be able to see you from our balcony, no problem. Told you you'd like it here! So much more freedom to play than in our old flat."

Above me, through the roof slats in the den, I spy the woman climbing. "Let me test the weight of the branches first," she says. "Better than a garden, Orla! From up here you can see... Someone's started cutting a path. Looks like it could lead all the way to the school railings – then across the Rec – handy! It's only a hop and a skip to walk you into school. But look at this lovely little wild patch!" She stretches out, holding on to two sturdy branches, and her voice changes like she's talking to herself. "All the fiery colours... I knew we'd love it here!"

After a while I hear her clamber down and now her shadow's above me, circling in small arcs.

"My turn!" the girl shrieks and the swing circles wider and wilder. The ravens set off shrieking too and their raucous cries fuse with the girl's laughter.

Slowly the woman's voice fades away.

Above, the sun dazzles as a bright yellow orb circles faster and faster. I scramble out to see her raven-black hair unravelling as the sun spins light all over Greenlands. I stare at the screeching, swirling dervish who whirls before me, dumbstruck until the golden vision settles into a skinny girl in yellow dungarees, two baby teeth missing and big teeth pushing through her gums just like mine are. She jumps off the swing, hands on her hips. First thing I notice close up are her eyes – green like tree moss.

"Where did *you* come from?" she asks.

"I live here!"

"What? In the wood?"

"Sometimes here and sometimes there!" I tell her, pointing from our den up to our balcony.

"Same!" She nods towards the flat above ours where her mum's already leaning over the balcony, chatting to my dad below. They both wave at us.

"I live here too now! Want a go?" she asks, handing me the knotted end of the rope swing.

I must be gawping. Can't speak.

"Aren't you going to say your name? It's polite to indruce yourself. What you staring at?" she asks, feet planted. "Can't you say your name?" She huffs, impatient.

"Kai!"

"Kai!" She echoes my name back at me.

This is my memory, probably false, but the sun bathed me at that moment and I felt like it was the first time I'd ever really heard my name.

I take the rope from her and climb on the knotted end. She runs round me with it, faster and faster, laughing when it's twisted as high and as taut as her strong, skinny arms can make it…

"Rude! You didn't ask me *my* name," she says, all wound together, her face close to mine now. I see myself reflected in her eyes and the wood behind and I can smell her minty toothpaste-breath.

"Orlaaaaaa," she sings, releasing her name with the swing.

"Orlaaaaaaaaaaaaaaaaaaaaaaaaaaaaaa," I let rip as I spiral through the air, holding her name till the end of my breath, filling my lungs with oxygen, mesmerized by our spinning orbit.

I turn and look up to Orla's balcony window, even though I know it's closed. I can't decide if writing this is making the summer pass faster or slower.

These are things I never noticed before I started writing. How the sun falls in shafts, stippling velvety orange through the silvery-blue leaves of Sula's eucalyptus tree. The colours are surreal. I take a photo for Om because he's not back from the art studio yet and I know he'd want to paint this.

Now that golden Orla day is all lit up in me as I write us in, just as we were... So much of me longs to leave us there.

I send the photo to Om and a few minutes later a message pings into my phone.

This is good. You are seeing beauty. This turning season is of use for your story. Colours are good also.
I will paint something of this.

But Om isn't in our Greenland's picture yet. The bomb had not yet dropped on his world far, far away, destroying his home and bringing him here.

It was still just the three of us. There had been no real bombshells yet for me, Zak and Orla. "The three musketeers," as Dad insisted on calling us, no matter how much I begged him not to treat us like kids.

Bow pecks around at my side and I catch myself almost

slipping into old habits and talking to her again, but I get a hold. I've seen Om a few times recently, but with Orla and Zak away at summer camp it's starting to kick in how much I miss us all being together.

It's got a bit chilly now but that's not the reason I'm shivering, actually shuddering as I look up to the roof of our Greenlands flats. I feel as if I'm standing on the edge of a precipice, taking this step back into the Bothy. Dad's right – it is hard to face yourself sometimes, as I was … as I have been. Back then, so full of embarrassment, fear that he would shame me. I'm charged with a mix-up of all that crap now, writing this. Something in me knew that, although everyone laughed and loved Dad's quirky ways, things were falling apart... Maybe that's why I was so desperately seeking sunshine.

We're crouched in the den, the three of us, beside the rope swing. Crouched because we've grown and our den hasn't. We're almost in Year Seven and we look ridiculous; clinging on to childhood, making our pacts of how whatever happens when we go to secondary we'll always stick together, look out for each other.

"It doesn't matter. Even if we get put in different

classes, we can still meet here after school every day," Orla reassures us as we crawl out of our den and look down over Ravenscroft Secondary. Our old den might have shrunk but each time I look at the enormous school buildings, half old, half new, their shadows seem to grow.

"Shame the path isn't cleared to the Rec railings! We could be at school in minutes!" Orla gazes down the hill. "We could clear it ourselves, if your dad's too busy."

"I told you. We can't. He doesn't want us to, says it's dangerous!"

"All right! No need to get all edgy!" Orla shrugs. "Just thought we could wake up later instead of having to drag ourselves round the roads."

"I'm not asking him again," I mumble.

Now Zak has to chip in. "If he's too busy I bet my mum and dad would help."

"I said no! Sorry. It's just Dad thinks of it as ours and he doesn't want anyone else using it as a cut-through."

"I mean, I get it, but it's not really finders keepers, is it!" Orla starts to argue but then she catches the dejected look on my face and changes her mind. "How about we clear it just enough to keep it as our secret passageway still? No one else would need to know..."

I turn away so they don't clock the tears in my eyes. No matter what we say about nothing changing I can feel it ...

everything already is.

"What's the matter, Kai?"

Orla always saw me, sometimes before I saw myself.

I'm cringing inside just as I did then, frozen and full of fire at the same time ... wanting to express something I had no words for.

Bow lays her head against my arm. How did I not notice before how old she's getting? Her torn wing trailing; thinner, frailer, less adventurous. She hardly flies at all any more except for my morning call. Sometimes, when I open my hands to her, she hops into my cupped palms and lets me cradle her.

She stirs, ruffles her wings and I set her down. I think she likes me sitting here day after day. I can feel the light pools opening up my mind as I write, clearing the path, and she's been here with me every step, flight and fall of the way. I gulp the freshening autumn air, letting the earthy scent of mulched leaves soothe me.

Zak doesn't give up easily, prodding me. "Remember when

I came back to yours and your dad brought us through this way. I loved it! We were wild that day."

"No!" I yell right in his face. I don't even know why I'm shouting but he backs away from me. "Dad says no. He says we have to let it wild up again … let it grow over or someone might find it and try to take it off us."

I see the look that Orla and Zak give each other. *Do they feel sorry for me, or Dad, or both of us?*

Orla nudges me and laughs. "Suit yourself! It was just an idea! I'll tell you what though, I'm not waiting around for you to make me late for school!" I know she's trying to lighten the mood.

Out of nowhere a dog barks close by and voices shock us into silence. Without saying a word we creep back inside our old den.

"Where are you going, Pops? There's nothing in there. It's just a bit of wasteland." A woman appears by an old man's side, attempting to pull him back to the path on the Rec below. Peering down the hill through the branch gaps, I see his skin, wrinkled as old bark.

At first I thought it was the dog whimpering, but it's the man. We're huddled together, our noses pressed up against the stick slats. The dog's snuffling the air and for a moment I think it's going to sniff us out, but it trots back to the old man's side.

The man starts to speak – his voice raspy, like every word scratches his throat. "I know it's here! It's got to be here! It was the first wee bothy I built! The corvids ken it." At first I think he's speaking another language until I strain closer and make out his Scottish lilt, like Mum's when she talks about where she grew up.

"Come on, Pops, you're getting all confused. There are no bothies in London. You've never lived here before. Remember you've come to stay with us. We're not in the Highlands any more," the woman reasons, taking the old man by the crook of his arm and gently leading him away.

"I need to go home, please let me go home, Kath!" the old man cries like a child.

"Don't upset yourself, Pops. Let's get you back inside. You need to rest now. The ground's too uneven here – you don't want another fall…"

We listen to their fading voices and watch the woman guide the old man slowly, pulling back branches to shield his eyes as they find their way out through the bottom railings on to the Rec.

"Poor old man. Maybe your dad's right about keeping this our secret! We don't want just anyone coming up here," Orla says, and I want to spring a hug on her like I used to do.

"What's a bothy anyway?" Zak asks, checking it out on his phone. "According to this, some kind of shelter left unlocked that anyone can stay in –" He reads on. "Used by anyone, but mostly gardeners and labourers on Highland estates."

"Sounded like he was really lost in his head," Orla says.

My phone pings. A text from Dad.

Scram's up!

"Gotta go!" I say, scrambling out as fast as I can so they don't see the river of tears running down my cheeks. Because somehow I know that after today, whatever any of us have vowed, things are changing and none of us can stop it.

The sun's just rising and a mist covers the tops of the Greenlands trees. I'm standing on the balcony with Dad. I can hear an old man calling through the mist. "Cassie, Cassie!" he cries over and over again, and I turn to Dad and I tell him how the old man is searching for a place he came to when he was a boy, that we should go back with the cutters and find it.

Why did we give up, Dad?

He shakes his head and says, "It's a mistake to go back. Don't go back, Kai. There's nothing there for us." And then he starts whimpering and his face morphs into the old man's and I shout at him to stop changing but he can't and he sinks on to his hands and knees and cries and cries. No matter what I do I can't make him stop.

When I wake my pillow's drenched in tears and I know that I have to go and take a look... To see if there is something hidden underneath that wilderness that we haven't discovered yet.

It's the weekend. Dad's out. I tell Mum I'm meeting Zak at his place, fingers crossed behind my back, hoping she won't find out he's away on holiday. I wait till Orla heads out for athletics training and set out to Greenlands with Dad's cutters.

On my hands and knees, no overalls or goggles to protect me now, I crawl through the undergrowth, beyond our den to where the dog was sniffing, away from any path me and Dad have cut before... I'm moving forward but it feels like burrowing back in time. I'm cutting away with the sharp shears now, thinking of all the worries that have crept in since the days when me and Dad were Greenlands Guardians.

Before I know it I'm hacking at brambles, and it feels good to be clearing again. I'm making progress. The ravens

follow me through. The daylight's almost gone in here and suddenly I'm in a tunnel, too far in to go back now, even though I know I should.

A branch needles right into my eye. Flinching at the shooting pain and in a blurred haze I see two ravens swoop down, looking on, concerned for me. I can just make out the raven pair now hopping ahead through our old den, like they're leading the way. *Am I still dreaming?* My arms flail, and as I stand, slats of our den roof fall away. I trample them, scrambling on. As I follow the ravens deeper, tugging away at the undergrowth, a voice in my head guides me. *Carry on, Kai, clear the way and maybe one day Dad and Mum will dance again.*

The moment passes and my eye and head clear. I turn back to our half-dismantled den and make a vow to myself that I will *never* tell Orla or Zak or anyone I came here today, following the rantings of the old man's foggy memory and a twisted dream. They would think *I'd* lost my mind. But the ravens turn to me, encouragingly.

Look to the shine in their eye, Kai.
Look to the shine in their eye.

My eye still stings and waters but the haze has cleared. I hack through wildly, angry at myself for being so weird that

I'm following this useless dream, ignoring the scratches on my arms and ankles, bleeding. I'm about to give up when the cutters hit something solid. As I scrape the undergrowth away I discover a wooden door. The ravens disappear through an opening, black wings edging their way inside. Frantic now, I cut away, clearing the ground until I can ease the door open further. The smell of earth and damp and age is in my nostrils.

Dropping to my hands and knees once more, I crawl to where the raven pair sit in the centre of … what is this place? Some kind of bunker? No. More of a shelter growing out of the ground. And this is how, crouched in our wilderness, I find the old man's bothy. The way the ravens caw and hop on a yellow-stained camp bed together, it seems they've known this place forever. I sniff the air and see their droppings scattered everywhere. So this is their home.

There is a window on one side, the glass shot through. Cautiously I cut away at the ivy vine that's reaching inside and through it I spy the Ravenscroft railings. I've done what Dad did not want me to do and properly cleared the path through our wilderness. I wrap my arms round myself, staring at the ravens. Then I lay the cutters down, place both hands over my eyes and cry and cry and cry … and I don't even know why.

I try to replace the slats of our den roof as best I can but you can see the sky through it now. The ravens sit beside me, watching, and I wonder if it's them making me have these thoughts. *Maybe it's good that you can see the sky now, Kai. Not everything your dad says has to be true – maybe for him, but not for you.*

I need to get away from them messing with my head. Back home I hide the cutters in the cupboard and head for the bathroom, but Mum comes out of their bedroom and bumps into me. "What's the matter with your eye, Kai? It's all bloodshot. And you're covered in scratches!"

"Got a boot to the head playing footie, so I took a short cut through Greenlands," I lie.

She shakes her head, wrinkles her nose and plants a kiss on my forehead. "Hmmm… Reminds me of when you and Dad used to—" She breaks off midway and I wish she would finish what she wants to say but it's like she can't talk about happy times any more.

She lifts her hand to my eye and I swerve away. "Stop fussing, Mum, I'm OK!"

I lock the door and strip my clothes off, watching the steam fill the bathroom, limbs relaxing as I slowly immerse myself in the heat of stinging water. Time slides away.

I lather my hands and blow bubbles, each one growing larger as thoughts form. Should I tell Orla or Zak, or should I keep it to myself? I could go back and cover over the tunnel in the undergrowth I cut to the bothy. It wouldn't take long to grow over again.

But now I know it's there, I can't. There is no going back.

When I'm out of the bath and wrapped in a towel I pad straight to my bedroom to text Orla and she agrees to meet me at our den this afternoon. Zak's away for this last week of our holiday before secondary starts, and I don't know why him being gone makes me happy, but it does.

"What's different?" Orla says, peering up at the rearranged roof slats of our den. I shrug and she edges closer to me. "Kai! You've got blood in your eye."

"I scratched it on a stick looking for something... I cut through the brambles and there *is* a bothy! In there, like the old man said." I come straight out with it.

"You're such an idiot!" She laughs, thinking I'm joking, so I dismantle the slats at the back of our den and crawl on through, clearing away the camouflage cuttings I'd placed to cover up the new tunnelled path.

Orla just gawps at me, her moss eyes shining.

"Coming? Watch you don't get scratched up!" I warn and feel her following me.

We're inside the bothy before she speaks again. She's casting around the place, struggling to take it all in. "I thought you were joking... We should try to find that old man and tell him!" Then her mood changes and I can see the cogs of her mind whirring. "You know what ... it's dry in here. This could be our new den." She sniffs and pulls a face. "Stinks though. It would need some make-over. The den is falling apart anyway, and it's too small now we're off to secondary. We could meet here any time – even in winter." Orla's all sparkly now, jumping around, making plans.

"I think the ravens might have something to say about that. They live here too!" I say as they hop up to the door.

Orla stops and shakes her head at me. "Sorry, ravens, but you'll have to move on!" She squints at them as they sit on the mattress, staring up at us both. "You think they're together, like a couple?"

"How would I know?" I ask, but I do think that and now I'm wondering why Orla's asking me.

Orla looked like a painting just then, her eyes shining with excitement, the warm, soft light on her skin and hair. I pause to truth-check myself – did I really feel this for her back then? Yes, I'm sure I did. Let me freeze life here when we were building something again from scratch. Not me and Dad any more, but me and Orla... And then she had to go and spoil it.

"Wait till we show Zak when he's back from his holiday!"

I want it to be just me and Orla and I feel guilty about that, so I don't tell her. But I'm happy that she doesn't argue with me when I say it feels like it should just be me and her dismantling our den. And so we do, silently, slat by slat, taking down what we had built, leaving only an arch leading to our new Bothy den. I see the tear-shine in her eyes as piece by piece we say goodbye to all the childish games we used to play.

As we walk back home she's chattering on about all the work there is to do to clean out the Bothy but all I can think of now is how I'm going to break it to Dad that our old den's gone and I've cut through. Just how he didn't want me to.

But when I get in Mum and Dad are curled up together on the sofa like they never are these days. Dad has his hand on Mum's belly... Mum's swollen belly. Something's changed. I know it. The light in their eyes is sparking bright now as they reach out for me to sit between them.

"Should I wash my hands?" I ask, holding them up to show the dirt under my nails.

"Don't worry about that!" Mum laughs and she takes a hold of my grubby hand, placing it on her bright white T-shirt. "We've been waiting to give you the news, Kai... You're going to have a baby brother or sister."

"When?" I ask, staring at my hand on the curved bulge of Mum's belly.

"January, we think!"

I felt like that was the first day of a new life. I felt like Mum and Dad loved each other again. I heard the music between them. I felt like somehow my wishing so hard for the baby and cutting through the wilderness had something to do with their happiness and from this point on everything was going to be OK.

The next day I take Dad down to show him the Bothy. He frowns when he sees our dismantled den but nods and says, "Well, son! We can build a new den for your brother and sister when they're old enough…" Above us a thrush bursts into song. Dad squeezes my shoulder. "Time for new nest-building – and for you too, Kai, to set out on your own path!"

"Dad!" I squirm away from him, embarrassed, even though our only witnesses are ravens.

I'm nervous but he's in such a good mood – whistling! I haven't heard him whistle since we were building the old den and somehow that makes everything feel right.

Once we're inside the Bothy he laughs and holds his nose. "Fancy this being hidden here all this time. Whiffs a bit! Raven crap!" He sniffs, inspecting the old camp bed. "Bit creepy, but no one's slept here in a long time. You'll have to make it safe and clean. Maybe even get your own lock on the door. I can fix the basics up for you." He peers through to the railings of Ravenscroft. "And remember, you should keep the path up to here secret. Don't cut those brambles down or you'll have everyone wanting a piece of this place."

"OK, Dad, we will," I say, and he wraps me in a bear hug.

"I'm sorry if I've been … distant, far away. I still can't get my head around you going off to secondary school, son. Come on then, let's fix up this bothy!"

Orla arrives just as Dad comes back with his tool kit. Me and Orla sweep out and disinfect while Dad clambers up on the roof, clearing the ivy and fixing the leak he's found that's making the place smell damp.

"Right then! I'll leave the decoration to you three musketeers!"

"Dad!" I groan, catching Orla's eye. "Zak's not even here!"

"Two musketeers then!"

I push him out of the door he's just fixed. He knows I'm only joking.

"That's all the thanks I get! All right, all right! I'll leave you alone." He laughs, peering up the open path that leads through our old den arch and up the steep slope to the balconies of Greenlands.

"Just so you know, I've cleared the sightlines so no mischief in here when you start secondary school. We can see what you're getting up to down here!"

Out of the corner of my eye I catch Orla blushing-up bright red and I stare Dad out. But I can't be angry with him for long because he trails off, whistling, and when Dad whistles I'm happy.

Mum's doing what she calls "nest-building". Every day, when she puts something out to recycle, we grab it for our Bothy. It's more like nest-clearing than building. Like she's cleaning out her old nest and we're the ones building a new one, and I think that's what we've done clearing out of our old den and setting up in the bothy. So far we've got a scrap of soft green carpet to cover the hard stone floor, a little chest of drawers to put games in and two bean bags.

When Mum comes down to see what we've done she smiles. "Home from home!" She places her hand on her stomach like it's a home too... I suppose it is for my brother or sister. I try to imagine a tiny baby swimming around inside her but I stop because it just feels too strange.

"Good to see you all set up but I don't think I'll be making the trip down here again." I take Mum's arm and help her climb the hill, though she makes out she doesn't need me to.

"I'm pregnant, not ill, Kai!"

But I notice how carefully Mum walks, like she's really afraid of falling.

Me and Orla were so busy building our own little Bothy nest those last few days of summer that I hardly thought about starting secondary until suddenly we're walking through those tall metal gates.

School's OK actually. The first few weeks are fine, despite getting lost a few times. Once I get confused with the timetable and turn up to the wrong lesson but it's Zak's mum teaching so she shows me where to go.

I always look for Orla but work out it's only at lunch break we can get together. Zak lucked out as usual and is in the same form as Orla. I wish it had been her and me … but it's fine, I suppose. There are other people I know from primary but I'm not after making new friends. Mostly I just wait for the end of school, till we can play footie on the Rec pitch and head to our Bothy.

Dad doesn't come down here much once me, Zak and Orla start hanging out. Every day that goes by I watch Mum's belly swell and as it does the happiness at home grows too. We are dancing through the days like we used to.

So everything's kind of all right. I don't love school and once or twice I've got into trouble for not paying attention, but I don't bother Mum or Dad with that, because at the end of the day I kick the stress away with Zak in a game of footie or a wrestling match. And sometimes I talk to Orla about stuff, if I need to.

With Dad it's enough for me to feel him near, listening to the strains of his sax dancing down the hill, sounding more confident each day. Most of the time I don't want him to but sometimes, just sometimes, I wish he would come to the Bothy too so we could be together like the old times. But he's so happy that he doesn't even mind putting on his raven suit for work. "Needs must," he tells me cheerily, "when you're saving up for a new baby."

It's like time's speeding up and every day the baby grows I feel like I'm growing too, then before I know it I'm sitting next to Dad, looking at the screen where the being that looked like a chick has grown into something that's more like my baby sister. Last scan she was doing a slow somersault around Mum's belly – this time Mum says there's no room. Mum's milky skin is all stretched and covered in lines as if the baby's drawing a map on her.

Mum's staring at the scan now, clasping Dad's hand. She can read the screen better than us because she's a nurse. The last time it took me ages to spot the alien chick, but even I can see now…

"Our girl!" Mum takes a deep breath as the doctor moves the scanning thing over her belly. "And you're sure everything's OK?" Mum's forehead's all worry-wrinkled.

"Absolutely normal."

A sister. Tears hit this page as hard as rain, heavy rain, and Bow hops by my side.

I don't even need to look at Mum and Dad to feel the happiness pouring out of them. Dad bends and gives Mum a long kiss like he's forgotten anyone else is in the room. They're dancing to their silent music again and I wish I were small enough to squish between them and sway on their feet. Dad bursts into song, "And I think to myself, what a wonder—"

"Dexter!" Mum laughs and pushes him away as she props herself on her elbows. "So what do you think, Kai?"

I turn my head to the side. "She looks more human than bird now," I admit and as I say that her bony fist boxes at me! "She's waving!" I laugh and I stretch out my arms and attempt a slow back bend, kicking into a somersault like she did last time I saw her floating around.

"No acrobatics in here, Kai!" Mum shields her stomach but she doesn't see that I'm only dancing to cover up the rush of love and happiness pulsing through my blood. Because today is the first day I've let myself believe that I'm going to be a big brother.

I hide my head under Dad's arm, as if it's a protective wing.

Dad hugs me to him, ruffling my hair. "Nothing to be ashamed of, son … being in awe at the wonder of the world," he says, wiping our tears away. "You'll be a great big brother! Not that long now." Dad squeezes me to him hard enough for me to feel his heart beating through his jumper.

I hear footsteps and turn to see Om walking slowly towards me, giving me time. He must have seen me from his balcony where he's set up his easel, painting and drawing away as I write. So at least he doesn't feel that far away. In any case, it's never been about talking between me and Om. He places a hand on my shoulder and sits down beside me, glancing from the book to my tear-streaked face and then up to where Bow has settled on a silver-leaved branch.

He wraps his jacket round me. "Don't you get cold sitting here for so long?"

I shake my head. "I need to write on."

He nods. "I understand. Zak and Orla say they've been

calling you but you don't answer. They asked me to see if you are fine. Just use group message so they are not worried for you. It is natural after all," he says gently.

"I'll get in touch." I hold my notebook up. "I've just been lost in this."

"I understand. Sometimes when you work you must be alone." Om taps his own chest. "But you are keeping in balance?" He turns his artist gaze upon me, his eyes like searchlights. "I too have been creating work for my portfolio. I think we are in the same space. But I have hardly seen you. Aunt Gisou invites you to eat with us one day."

"Thank you. Thank her. I will." And my stomach rumbles loudly remembering the last feast she made.

"Your stomach agrees!" Om laughs.

I try to smile through my tears but it's not that convincing. I blow a deep breath out, flicking through all the words I've written… It's true, I've hardly noticed time passing since I've been writing. I haven't even missed Orla as much as I thought I would. It's like I've been away too long and the deeper I get into it the more obsessed I am. If I could sit here all day and night I would. But now … it's just getting too raw. "I don't know if I should go on with this writing or not. What if I really get lost again? Is it even good for me?"

Om leans forward and picks up a fistful of earth from around the trunk of Sula's tree. It's full of dense clay clods that he works away at till they're fine enough to sift between his fingers.

He stands and points to the easel set up on his balcony. "Sometimes I think the only thing we can do is work through. You are not alone." He rubs his hands together to clean them. "After everything is lost one thing that cannot be taken from me is my painting. Same with your writing. If you want sometimes we can sit together here and create our work," he says, smiling gently.

I let him rock me, like he did once before, and this shredding grief pours out of me again.

The next part was the time of bliss so how can it be the hardest part to write? The time when everything was going to be put right. It was also the time when me and Orla were changing ... when I loved her most.

We're hanging out on the bean bags in the Bothy, duvets wrapped round us to keep warm, when I tell Orla that the baby's a girl and for the first time in ages she springs a hug on me. "I'll have one of each!"

"How? I didn't know you had a brother?" I ask. Orla never

talks about her dad. Says she's never met him and she never wants to after he left her mum when he heard she was pregnant.

She narrows her eyes and squints at me then jabs her finger into my chest. "You idiot, I mean *you*! You're the closest to a brother I'll get because Mum says she's not having any more children, even if she does ever meet the love of her life."

This is the moment I realize how she sees me – my gut twists and I tune out till she nudges me.

"Are you even listening? My mum says she can be your mum's midwife!"

"Yeah, I know – that's weird!"

"So when *do* we get to meet our sister?!"

"It's supposed to be fifth of January but Mum was late with me – she says it was like I wanted to stay in the warm because it was snowing so heavily when I was born."

"I love snow!" Orla's eyes sparkle.

I want to reach out and touch the smooth skin on her neck. Sometimes I just want to stare into her eyes. Sometimes, like now … I want to kiss her.

"You will let me be her sister too, won't you?" Orla begs.

I nod, not trusting myself to open my mouth.

"We've got till then to make this hovel a palace in her honour!"

"We already have," I say, looking around.

"It's OK but still a bit grim in here. The walls are scuzzy and cold. We should paint it! Make it sunny even in winter!" Orla shivers and blows a puff of ice breath into the air. "Maybe one day we could have her birthday party here! Build a fire out there…"

The ravens set to screeching on the roof above us.

"I wish they'd bog off though! Don't care what you say, they give me the creeps."

"We did take over their home!"

"What are you on about?"

"Dunno, I feel a bit sorry for them now that we've sealed the window and the door. Maybe they're watching over us," I mutter, listening to their deafening cries.

"You're such a weirdo, Kai! Birds are *meant* to live in trees!" Orla laughs, nudging me. "Don't you dare let them in, after all the work we've put into this place. I'm not having them crapping over everything." She crinkles her nose. "Zak's right, I can still smell them in here! Can't you?"

I shake my head but Orla's wandering around, sniffing in the corners. "It's still a bit earthy in here. If we paint the walls it might help. You couldn't bring a baby in here as it is."

"Not sure Mum would let us have the baby in here whatever colour we paint it."

"Well, she won't stay a baby forever, will she? She'll grow!"

Orla's on a roll, sparking with energy, eyes shining like emeralds. "We've got some leftover paint from my room. Let's do it today! To celebrate! So we'll never forget the day we knew we were getting a sister!" Then she's off, sprinting up the hill, calling back to me to pull everything away from the walls so we can get started.

Orla mixes the paint and goes to hand me a brush, but hesitates. Her icy-cold skin brushes mine. "I know!" She grins, plants her hand in the tray of bright yellow paint and nods for me to do the same. My head swirls with the fumes, or maybe it's being this close to Orla as we print our palms on the Bothy wall. Her left hand, my right.

"It's so bright we'll need sunglasses in here now!" I joke.

"We can pretend we're with Zak, sunning ourselves in St Lucia with his family for Christmas!"

"I bet you wish you were!" It just slips out … and bitterly.

Orla's eyes dull and her lips tense in a straight line. "You've got to stop doing that, Kai. We stick together, remember. We promised… Forever."

Then she breaks into a grin. "I've got an idea. So we'll always remember!" And with another swoop of her brush she paints over our handprints. "We'll always know our sunshine selves are here!" She smiles and we are quiet for a while, bathed in yellow and dazzled just like I was the first day I ever saw Orla swirling above the den. "Come on, Kai. I'm not doing all the work! What are you staring at? Have I got paint on my face?"

"No! Nothing," I say, carrying on. "Just don't tell Zak our handprints are underneath."

Orla pauses. "Why?"

"I dunno! Just thought he might feel left out."

Orla shrugs. "He doesn't think that way. In any case, I'm not sure he's into the Bothy like we are. He liked our old den better. I think he was actually a bit pissed at us for taking it down without him. He thinks it's spooky in here…" Orla stands back to admire our work. "Maybe he'll like it better now!"

I hope not… Do you think of Zak as a brother too, Orla? I try to push that question to the back of my mind.

"Just don't say, about our hands, OK?"

"OK, OK!"

We made a pact that day.
That come what may,
even though anyone's supposed to be free to shelter in a bothy,
this one belongs to us.
And us alone.

All through that Christmas holiday it felt like summer in our Bothy. Even when we were half frozen to death, huddled in coats, hats and glove, snuggled under a duvet, we were cosy, wrapped in our secret sunshine while we waited for who Orla was already calling "our sister".

"Kai! Didn't you hear me calling?" My heart leaps. I drop my pen and it rolls towards Orla's feet. She picks it up and hands it back to me.

"Thought you weren't coming back till Om's exhibition day."

She raises her hands to her hair, self-consciously. "I got the weekend off! For your birthday – haven't missed one yet," she says. I can hear in her voice she's trying not to make a big deal of it. "I messaged you so many times! You could have texted me." She sits down beside me and I do a double take.

"Sorry! Your hair looks great – suits you! How's summer camp going anyway? How's Zak?" I ask, pulling myself together.

"Haven't seen much of him. It's hard work coaching

the kids. I only see him in the canteen. Football and athletics are on different campuses. Maybe you should have come with us…"

Biting her lip, she turns, glancing up at Om's balcony and suddenly I get it. "Om called you, didn't he?"

She carries on gnawing at her bottom lip. "He was worried about you and I felt like I forced you into the writing by going on about it and getting you that notebook." She peers at the last words on my page. "You could at least join in on the group chat."

"Just doing what we said we should! Give each other space!" I shrug. "Anyway, it's easier this way."

Just then Om comes out on his balcony, waves and goes back inside. "So you *have* got Om spying on me?"

She places one of her hands in my palm and curls her fingers tightly round mine, shaking her head. "It's not like that! But he doesn't miss much. If you want to know he was worried about you … spiralling. He said he found you sitting in the cold and rain down here, crying your eyes out." Orla's own eyes are glassy with tears and she wipes them away. My chest clenches in emptiness. *I wish she could love me like I love her.* "Anyway, I've missed you both and Mum too. I wanted to get you a present but I'm broke." She lets go of my hand and wraps one arm round the spindly trunk of Sula's tree as if she's hugging her. Then she opens her palm and waits for me to place my palm against hers in our secret sunshine sign.

"That's where I was, lost in before... Painting our hands. You must have known!" I whisper.

I know I'm clinging to her, feeling her heart beat hard against mine, but I can't let go. She pulls apart first and bumps my arm. "Just don't give up, Kai." It's half plea, half order.

"I better go see Mum. Birthday drink at The Raven later?"

I nod. Something has settled again, seeing Orla, like the scattered pieces are floating back together again.

"You done now?" she asks, tapping my notebook as she gets up.

I shake my head. "I have work to do!"

She grins. How many times has she said that to me!

When you've known someone all your life everything feels like an echo.

I open my mouth wide and my jaw clicks with tension.

Just go there, Kai... Just go there. Do it now while you know Orla's not so far away.

Since my school report Mum's been worried about me. I don't know why she's making such a big deal. It was mostly OK but had a few 'room for improvements' mainly because Salter's had it in for me since we played that prank of bringing salt in. Every time he turned round we'd throw it over our shoulders so the floor would always be covered in salt. It wasn't even my idea but when he fell flat on his face, skidding out the door, I laughed the loudest so since then he's had it in for me.

What Dad says is true… I'm the youngest in my year, but it's like they still have to take me out in front of everyone. Like they see me as this big threat when half the time I'm just going along with what everyone else is doing. I'm sorry I caused an argument between Mum and Dad though – Dad shouting the odds about how he won't see his son put through the same racist shit that he was and Mum saying he shouldn't jump to conclusions, and that I should have more respect for my teachers. They haven't argued in ages. I wish I'd steered well clear of the Salter prank and, right now, I decide – I'll try to make it up to them.

Mum's got it into her head that I've been spending too much time in the Bothy and we need "special family time" before the baby comes. But Dad's worried and I am too that she's wearing herself out.

I watch her blowing ice circles. Frost hovers over the river like it will never lift. To be honest I wish we didn't have to come on this "last outing" as Mum calls it.

I miss Dad coaching us. I know he's too busy with extra shifts at work now but when he does come down to see us train on a weekend I see this look of surprise cross his face like he's seeing me for the first time.

Last weekend it was swimming. When Mum came out of the changing rooms I couldn't believe the size of her belly. *This is finally happening!* While Mum was floating on her back, and Dad was swimming lengths, I saw the baby move and Mum took my hand and placed it on her belly. It was the weirdest feeling. "Not long now, Kai!" Mum smiled.

It weirded me out so I kicked my own somersault turn in the water.

This week's "quality time" is Dad's choice but as Mum's slowed down so much now, puffing her breath into the icy air, I think it might have been easier if we'd just gone swimming again.

From the way Dad is around her I think he wishes he hadn't suggested this outing either. "Stop fussing. I'm feeling fine. You two go on the tour. I'll be happy sitting here!" Mum reassures us but Dad's not keen to leave her.

"I'll call if I need you. I can't believe we've never even brought Kai to the Tower! Go on, the tour's starting soon."

Now we're here Dad does actually seem excited about meeting whoever this Ravenmaster is, so I'm glad I didn't complain! I get why he chose the Tower of London because ravens have always been part of the chat between me and Dad. I would have loved this when I was a kid but not now. Sometimes I think Dad and Mum have been so caught up in watching the baby grow, they haven't got a clue how much I've changed since I started at secondary.

"Is Ravenmaster an actor?" I ask, checking out his black and red outfit with puffball sleeves and velvet trousers. He looks like he's just walked out of Shakespeare's time. When Dad asks if he doesn't get a bit tired of dressing up like that every day he looks offended.

The Ravenmaster is definitely not an actor. When he shows us round the old stone buildings you can tell how much he loves the ravens, like they're his children. "Now please respect the rules of the Tower and follow my instructions. Anyone want to help me feed them?" he asks.

Dad always gets wound up whenever there's anyone like a teacher around. I think me being in trouble at school has got to him. I will him not to go off on one now, but I can tell by the look in his eye he's about to. "Loves himself a bit, doesn't he? Thought this was supposed to be a bit of fun, not a lecture!" Dad mumbles.

He's embarrassing me so I step forwards and say, "Yeah! I'll help." And while I do I tell the guide about the ravens of Greenlands, how there's this pair that stick together.

"They're loyal all right! Us humans could learn a few lessons from them. The divorce lawyers wouldn't make such a killing if humans were all as loyal as ravens!" The Ravenmaster laughs at his own joke, directing it towards the group of accompanying adults.

Dad sneers and I pull a face at him to stop. I'm old enough to get the attempt at a joke and the polite laughter of all the other adults except for Dad who has gone sullen and shrunk back into himself. I don't see why he looks so uncomfortable. I should be the most embarrassed because I am definitely the oldest kid here!

I wish the Ravenmaster hadn't said that word "divorce", because it gets me thinking how I used to worry if Mum and Dad would stay together before we knew about the baby. I'd forgotten how much I used to worry about that.

After I've fed the ravens I join Dad again, hanging back, looking in the opposite direction to the Ravenmaster. "Are you and Mum going to get married after the baby's born?" The words just slide out of me.

Dad nods. "We never bothered much about that stuff before but your mum says she wants to in a year or so.

It won't be anything showy though! We were thinking maybe we could deck out our Greenlands wood and the Bothy and have a little party down there."

I take Dad's arm. "Sorry I made you and Mum argue. I won't get into any more trouble, promise. You are both happy again?" I ask.

He wrinkles his forehead like he's surprised I noticed they weren't and places an arm round my shoulder. "Ignore me. It's my shit. You know how school winds me up! Last time me and your mum were this happy was when you were born, son!"

I pull away. "Orla wants to be a bridesmaid. Can she?"

Dad laughs. "I expect so!"

I hardly hear what the Ravenmaster's going on about now. I'm trying to imagine us all a year older at Mum and Dad's wedding with the baby maybe even crawling. And maybe by then I'll pluck up the courage to tell Orla how I feel.

I'm off on one now, picturing it in my mind. The wood's all lit up with fairy lights, Dad playing his sax. People dancing. Me and Orla in the Bothy, cushions everywhere. She's wearing a bright yellow dress of course and finally I pluck up the courage to—

"That doesn't sound right. You mean they don't ever try to fly free?" Dad's voice cuts into my daydream.

The Ravenmaster stares at Dad, obviously annoyed at

the interruption. But he pauses for a moment, working out how to answer. Then he starts with some complicated explanation about how they clip the wing feathers. I think of the ravens of our wilderness and the thought of it makes me cringe, but he reassures everyone that it's not cruel because they only clip them on one side so they're unbalanced enough that they don't fly far. "See! They'll flutter over to the castle walls and then land again. They sense where the boundary lies."

Dad starts to twitch. The muscle in his cheek is pulsing. I haven't seen him like this for ages. "It's all right, Dad!" I try to calm him but he's getting fidgety, shifting from foot to foot as the Ravenmaster sits on a low wall and ushers us close. "Let's go!" I beg, pulling Dad's arm, but he's rooted to the spot, this grim, hard-lined look on his face like he's spoiling for a fight.

"Legend has it that if the ravens leave the Tower then the kingdom will fall," the Ravenmaster announces, all solemn.

Dad scoffs in disgust and starts on an under-his-breath rant. Some of the parents with younger children step away from us.

"Dad, let's go. Mum might need us," I say and that seems to bring him back to himself. He lets me pull him away but not before he's shouted back loud enough for everyone to hear.

"If the kingdom can only stand by clipping wings, then

let the blasted thing fall!"

"Dad! Don't get upset," I plead. "Stop getting worked up. Everyone's staring at us!"

"What do I care? Let them stare!"

If I could have found this hill to look down on this moment from. If I could have known then what I know now... Maybe I would have told someone about the shadows I saw, but didn't understand, haunting my dad that day and, in truth, other days before. If Mum or Dad or I had told someone about the shadow times maybe I could have stopped our tower falling. What would I say to my twelve-year-old self if I could reach across time to that day? Tell someone, Kai. Tell Mum, tell Orla, tell Zak what you're worried about. But tell them what? Dad's talking in a way I don't understand? How can you tell someone something you can't even put into words?

On the way to the café Dad won't stop ranting on about how cruel it is, what they do to the ravens. "Surprised the animal rights people aren't on to it, but I suppose if they're the Queen's ravens they can do what they want. Same old story."

I try to calm him down before we get to Mum because she hates it when he goes off on one about the royal family and I don't want them to get into another argument about something so stupid so I ask if they've decided on names for the baby and he says, "Not yet, though we've got a few ideas." But he doesn't tell me what they are. He's still a bit wired when we get to the table where Mum's sitting, her head in her home birth book. "Don't tell your mum what they do to the wings; it might upset her," Dad confides in me.

"The Ravenmaster said it doesn't hurt them, Dad. And he did say he loved the ravens like they were his children."

"I wouldn't want to be his children, if that's what he does to them."

"There you are! Hungry?" Mum asks, handing me some money. Her eyes dart from Dad to me. "Get another pot of tea and some cake, if you want. Choose some for us too."

She's already clocked Dad's edginess and only asks me to go so she can calm him down. As soon as I walk over to the counter she pulls Dad aside and starts whispering. Most of it I can't hear but I know what that clenched jaw means. They're huddled together, talking for ages. Luckily the queue's long.

When I eventually come back balancing the tray Dad stands up and takes it from me. I can see he's more or less himself again. "Sorry for getting all worked up, Kai!" Dad says, tapping my arm. "All that talk of unbalancing wings kind of got to me!"

Mum turns her head away so I can't see how upset she is. I know Dad had a tough time when he was growing up, but sometimes I wish he'd talk about it – what it was like for him in care and why he hates everything about school – instead of bottling it up.

When Dad goes to clear the tray away Mum winks at me and smooths her hands over her stomach. "Don't worry yourself about Dad, Kai. Just last-minute nerves!"

On the way home, walking along the river, I take one of Dad's arms and one of Mum's and I realize that it's probably the last time we will walk together for a while, just the three of us.

The ice mist has lifted and the Christmas lights are shining, reflecting a million stars on the water. A neon sign blasts out Happy New Year wishes and Dad points to where you can see the spire and dome of St Paul's rising above the heavy winter fog. "We should have gone there instead. I've always wanted to go inside. Why have we never been, Janice?"

Mum's eyes light up. "Let's come next Christmas then,

with this little one?"

Dad wraps his arm round Mum's waist, or tries to. "It's a date! By then I should be able to get my arms all the way round you!" he jokes, and she bats him away, laughing. Dad's humming again to 'There is a Green Hill Far Away', his favourite hymn. "Do you think you can put in requests?" he asks, laughing.

As I fall asleep Dad's old chant is in my ear and I know it isn't the ravens I am afraid of any more...

Don't fear the ravens, Kai.
Look to the shine in their eye.
See how the light glints on their feathers,
painting rainbows on ebony wings.

I wake up with a heavy head and Dad's voice singing, deep with foreshadowing.

Shaving, I inspect myself in the mirror, trying to work out what Orla sees. I shouldn't let the stubble grow.

I see it in people's glances, the worry that I'm letting things slide again. Last time we drank at The Raven was just after they'd done their last exams. I didn't stay long because I had nothing to celebrate and Om couldn't come so me and him ended up back at his flat drinking his aunt's cinnamon tea instead.

Orla calls for me. That's the thing I always used to like about living on the first floor – people have to pass you, so you get collected!

"You look better!" Orla smiles when I open the door.

I nod. "Stubble free in your honour!"

I can't get used to how different she looks with her hair short. She walks ahead of me and I want to reach out and touch the indent at the bottom of her neck.

She links arms with me as we head along the road towards The Raven. "How's it going with the kids?"

"Good! I work with them in the holiday club in the morning and write in the afternoons. When I've felt like giving up on the writing they've kept me going. They're kind of the motivation to sort myself out. Some of them remind me of how I was at that age and, I dunno... It feels like writing out what happened might be some kind of use in the end, and not just for me or us. Anyway, working with them has got me thinking about what I'm going to do when I finally leave this place!"

We're a couple of beers in, after Orla's embarrassed me with her usual terrible out-of-tune rendition of 'Happy Birthday', when she breaks it to me that she's got something to tell me.

I take a swig of beer and zone out. If it's what I think it is I would rather not know.

"Maybe I'll indruce you one day!"

I frown, not understanding... As if I need introducing to Zak!

Orla ruffs her hair up, forgetting she's cut in a fringe and smooths it down again. "Chidi, her name's Chidi."

I try to look unfazed while I take this in and just about manage a smile as Orla chatters on.

"What's she like?" I manage.

Orla takes out her phone and shows me a photo of her and a tall girl with their arms slung over each other's shoulders. "You look happy!"

"We are. I don't know her that well yet but I really like her... She's another trainee coach."

I nod, taking sips of my beer because I keep thinking of things I want to ask her, but I'm not sure I should or can.

Orla giggles. "I can practically read your mind, Kai. Do me a favour, will you? When you're sitting there, working life out according to Kai, think about this – you don't know everything about me! We don't even know everything about ourselves yet, none of us do. It's like Zak's mum says, 'We're all a work in progress.'"

I let Orla do the talking while my head stops spinning and somehow this news helps and finally I know I've got to stop clinging on to what's never going to be.

———

I wake up to Bow's dawn call and it propels me back down here to our Green Hill, bringing a sleeping bag with me so I don't get chilled. Now I hear Orla's laughter inside me and I'm watching the sky glow mad colours of yellows and oranges etched in slate-grey lines. I feel charged, like seeing Orla has given me space in my heart to write this out.

Om's already on his balcony, painting, capturing the dawn light rising. He salutes me and I salute him back as I sit by Sula's tree. He's doing his work, I'm doing mine, and I feel like he's literally got my back!

Now – when I see it on the page – the word *foreshadowing* actually makes me shudder. I wrote a whole essay about it in English that wasn't very good, but as I've started writing this I think I understand the point. Maybe the reason I never really got the grades I should have until now is because I couldn't *feel* these abstract concepts. What did

I care then about Hamlet's tragic demise! His fatal flaw...
But now ask me to write that essay and I could probably
ace it.

If I ever do get to be some kind of teacher I'll try to
find a way to explain a fatal flaw or how things stack up
before the character actually knows the earth's about to
shift under them. I'd get people to write out their own
foreshadowing, even if they didn't show their work to
anyone. Then they'd really get it when they read it in a
book or saw it in a film.

But I suppose, in life, if we actually paid attention to a
foreshadowing when we saw it there wouldn't be tragedies.
Because if we could spot the signs we would be able to stop
the story before the bad shit happened. I would end the
story by painting secret sunshine hands with Orla, when
there was only hope before us. But that's not the truth.

I push the notebook aside and close my eyes, letting
my mind wander.

"Kai?" Orla calls, coming up beside me. "You were miles
away again!"

Deep with foreshadowing.

"I'm off now!" She lays a little bunch of daisies by Sula's
tree. "I know you said your family weren't going to make a
thing of it but it *was* today, wasn't it? The day we planted
this tree? The day after your birthday?"

I nod, touching a silvery leaf.

"Just been to say goodbye to Om. You should drop in and see what he's working on… It's unbelievable!"

"What's he up to?"

Orla shakes her head. "Not sure. It's like he's painting being here, on Greenlands. It's not exactly here though… It's kind of somewhere else at the same time. There are ravens, and he's painted the old skyline of his city."

"Are they still all in black and white?"

"Mostly, but then there are these really bright flashes of colour. I sat next to him while he was painting. I think he might be a genius. Anyway, you're clearly both on a roll! How's the writing going today?" Orla smiles.

"Nothing genius about it but I'm doing it. There's no way I'll be able to finish this without you and Om filling in the gaps."

"We promised we would when you're ready, didn't we?" She sighs, peering at the words.

I offer her the book and hesitantly she takes it from me.

I lie on my back, cloud-gazing. It's the best time of year for it. Clouds at the end of summer are awesome. Today they're like a crinkled drift of brain across the sky. Bow's here at my side and, as I watch Orla read, I feel as if she's inside my mind and I don't suppose that really matters. Every now and then she looks over at me and smiles or sighs or cries. I don't know where she is in our story.

There's something unbearable about thinking that if it were a story that had not already been written there'd be so many times where we could rewind, rewire, reroute.

Orla turns over on to her belly and continues reading. She's almost got to where I finished off. My last words hanging in the air where she interrupted me.

Deep with foreshadowing.

"Look at me, Kai!" Her tear-washed eyes are so bright I can see myself in them.

"Stop being so hard on yourself. Forget about foreshadowings. You know how I always wanted to be Sula's sister. That can't be but I *can* be yours and you've got Om and Zak. They're your brothers too," she whispers and wraps her arms round me. "You've always got me." I feel a million arrows piercing at my heart. Because I know I have to let go of what I've longed for her to say… Maybe I'm finally hearing what she's always been trying to tell me – that she can never love me in the way I want her to.

She checks her phone. "Gotta go, Kai!" She eases herself up, leaning on my shoulder and kissing my cheek. "I love you, Kai."

"Love you too, Orlie!"

Now that I'm finally stripped of my longing, the hug she gives me feels like it used to when we were children. I have this strange urge to set up a swing where the old one was and ask Orla to push me on it, faster and faster... But I know that's the opposite of what I need to do if I'm ever going to slow down enough to look each twist and turn straight in the eye.

So much easier to go for the high. I sigh and sigh and sigh and, in the end, just pick up where I left off. I carry on because that's all I can do.

The outing to the Tower is the last we make. It gets so cold and Mum says we need to stay snug and cosy while we get on track for the baby coming any day now. I think she's looking out for Dad too, after how he was at the Tower.

It's stressing me out with all the cleaning and tidying and this great big blow-up pool thing that's arrived in the middle of our front room ready for the baby to be born in. I wish Mum would go into hospital instead of having the baby right here.

Mum and Dad are asleep and I think about calling up for Orla, but today I could do without her searching questions. With her mum being one of my mum's midwives she won't stop going on about it all and I just need to get away. I text Zak and we arrange to meet at the Bothy.

On the way down a song thrush is making such a racket that I veer off the path to investigate. It's trying to ward me off but I duck under the branches to find a pale blue egg shattered on the frozen earth. Halfway in and halfway out a tiny shrivelled bird with spindly limbs is lying on the ground. I bend down low to take a closer look and my stomach clenches.

It's just a bird that fell out of its nest ages ago, I remind myself.

A thrush,
a songbird,
fallen from its little low heaven.

"Little low heaven, little low heaven," I chant as I make my way to the Bothy, fending off the feeling in my belly that something else is broken.

It's just a bird falling out of a nest.

Happens all the time.

Little low heaven.

Little low heaven.

Little low heaven.

I bash at my temples to stop the pounding chant but I

can't get the picture of the shrivelled chick in its broken sky shell out of my mind.

By the time Zak turns up, I've got a hold of myself. "You all right?" he asks, getting his playing cards out and dealing.

We play Cheat and every so often the raven mates swoop down on to the roof. After we've played for a bit I think about telling Zak about the shrivelled chick I just buried at the top of the hill. I think about telling him about what my dad said about the Tower falling too, but every time I'm on the brink of talking I flush hot with something like shame. Zak loves my dad… Why can't I tell him? Somehow it would feel like a betrayal.

"Cheat!"

Zak calls me out and slowly I lay my cards down, exactly as I said they were.

But I never really did lay my cards on the table and Zak couldn't read me. I nearly always won but I suppose in the end I was always the loser, because maybe if I'd told him what was going on with my dad back then… What's the point? There's no flipping the pack … no going back and changing the course of history.

As Zak deals again the raven pair come hopping up to the Bothy door, closer than ever before. If Orla were here she'd shoo them away. "Sometimes they look like they know what I'm thinking!" I tell Zak, pushing the memory of the fallen chick from my mind.

He scuffs my arm and laughs. "Kai! *I* don't even know what you're thinking half the time!"

When did I shut you out, Zak?

"Kai! It's started!" Orla calls, her voice skipping through the air and moments later her feet are pounding down the track.

I want to call to her to be careful, not to disturb the thrush's egg buried at the top of the hill, but she's already skidding to a halt outside our Bothy, her face flushed with excitement. "Hi, Zak! Didn't know you were coming over!" She grins, happy to see us here together. "Kai! It's happening. Baby's coming. My mum's gone round to yours!" She judders out the words all in a rush. I can't take them in. "Anyway, Mum says it'll be ages yet so there's no hurry but if you like you can come up to our flat till she calls for us!" She wraps her arms round me and Zak in a huddle like she used to.

Only it's different, because I can feel the small, soft mounds of her breasts where there used to be only a hard, skinny ribcage. I pull away. *She* might think of me as her brother, but all I know is that hugging Orla these days doesn't feel like hugging a sister to me.

"Maybe we should all stay here," I say.

She laughs. "For a bit, if you like! But don't you want to hear what's going on?"

"Not really!" I say, pulling a face. "I wish she'd gone to the hospital. Dad does too," I mumble.

"Mum's delivered loads of babies at home. It's what your mum wants. It'll be all right. She couldn't have a better midwife…"

Little low heaven.
Little low heaven.
Little low heaven.

I used to blurt out the stuff that reels through my head to both of them, but then I never used to have so many worries. Now my best friends are leaning against the yellow wall and chatting, Orla's and my handprints at their backs – *has she forgotten?* It's the first time I feel this stabbing in my chest that I try to ignore because it makes me want to grab Zak and all the new things he's brought for the Bothy and throw him and them out…

I wish he would just leave us alone in our Greenlands home now. I know I asked him to come here but I can't stop this weird thought flashing through my mind. What's ours is his, but what's his isn't ours. How can that be right? How would he feel if we just ran across the Rec and showed up in his garden? This anger keeps flaring up in me like I've felt in Dad and even my thoughts sound more like Dad's than mine. I wish Zak would just get the hint and clear out now. Stick to his side of the Rec like the other kids in their big houses do and leave me and Orla to our little low heaven of Greenlands.

Maybe Zak can read me better than I thought because after a while he says he has to go. I say sorry for being quiet. It's because I can't concentrate on anything, thinking about Mum's in labour in our flat…

Zak hugs me the way our dads hug, patting each other hard on the back. I never used to think one thing about hugging Zak or Orla. It was like we were one tangled root of the same tree…

"Good luck, mate!" he calls as he leaves. Even the way we speak to each other sounds like we're rehearsing how to be when we've emerged out of the shell of childhood that we lived in for so long together. Since secondary it's all begun to crack open … but who are we kidding?

We've still got gunged-up wings and haven't yet learned how to fly together into a grown-up world.

"You two are so awkward with each other these days," Orla says. "Come on, I'll race you!" She sets off at a sprint up the hill. We run shoulder to shoulder, ducking through the den entrance and up, reaching the top of our Green Hill together and in this moment of racing with Orla I forget all about foreshadowings and broken skies.

I wish I could freeze time right there. I don't care how steep the hill is. I just wish we could have stayed like that, forever running together before Sula's tree was planted, when my lungs were free to breathe, when our way was open.

Breathless, clanking through the metal security doors, we head upstairs and past our flat where Mum is having the baby!

We sit in Orla's flat, listening to the sounds below. Once or twice we hear Dad playing his sax then stopping abruptly. The balcony door's closed but we can hear his

music rising up through the floor and suddenly I realize…
"Can you always hear us this clearly from up here?"

Orla shrugs. "Sometimes!"

I think of all the conversations we've had when Dad has been sad, when he rants and Mum closes the doors and windows. I wonder how much of them Orla and her mum have heard.

Orla says she's actually been to work with her mum to see a baby being born. She tells me how amazing it is, even though she felt a bit faint and didn't see the end bit.

"You mean the beginning!" I joke because however cool she's playing it, she's wincing at every alien moan that floats up to us. It doesn't even sound like Mum.

Orla ignores me and opens her balcony door but shrinks backwards. "Get away!" She flaps her arms at the ravens, to shoo them off. That's weird. They've never flown up to our balconies before. Now they're perching on Orla's railings, every so often hopping down to ours as if they're as nervous to know what's going on as we are.

"Good job Mum will be too busy to notice them! She thinks they're bad…" Orla purses her lips to stop herself carrying on.

"Bad … what?"

"They make a bad mess!" Orla shakes her head, not

wanting to speak the words that are running through both of our minds.

Bad ... luck, bad ... omens. Though the ravens don't worry me as much as the broken sky egg I buried today and can't bring myself to tell Orla about.

No matter how much she flaps and shoos, the ravens will not leave. Hopping backwards and forwards from our balcony to Orla's, their piercing eyes staring. I look to the shine in their eyes because I reckon if they could they would tell me what's going on. I think maybe the ravens in the Tower and their unbalanced wings have got to me, because somehow I feel closer to these Greenlands ravens than ever, like we belong together.

Dad's comforting music weaves up to us.

"Sometimes when your dad's playing the sax me and Mum just sit here on the sofa with the door open to listen." Orla closes her eyes and pats the seat beside her for me to sit too. "I like those in-between notes best, the ones that aren't sure of themselves, like they're reaching for something. Do you know what I mean?"

"I think so."

What I do know is right at this moment I want to reach for Orla, hold her face in my hands and kiss her. In the in-between notes when I almost do, I think she wants me to kiss her, but I wait too long and she opens her eyes as

Mum's moan turns into a roar. I wonder how it can be that people are born like this. How can it be so hard to be born? By the way Mum's crying out, it sounds more like something's dying.

Did I really wonder that? I think I did. I was reaching for the in-between notes Orla was telling me she liked best. I don't think adults give kids enough credit for hearing those in-between notes. Maybe some kids are more tuned into them than others but I was always feeling the pitch. That's the thing about Orla. She makes me dig deep into myself, search more. I've been reaching for those in-between notes for so long now. I suppose in writing this I'm still reaching.

"Hear that?" Orla springs up and quickly slides open the balcony door...

It is the sweetest raw sound I have ever heard.

Bird call,
not exactly.

Cry,
not exactly.

More like a cat's mewl.

With the first song of new life the ravens take flight into
the night.

Me and Orla hold our breath,
staring into each other's eyes.
No in-between notes left to sing or sigh,
she reaches out and kisses my lips,
fleetingly.

It felt like I had discovered a missing chord in me.

We go helter-skeltering downstairs and Dad flings
opens the door and grabs me in a bear hug, whispering
of miracles, not even a bit embarrassed about his hairy
chest in front of Orla whose laughter is in my ear.
Dad tells me to take my top off like he has so the baby
can smell me and know me. It feels weird, like

we're little moley creatures I've seen snuffling through the undergrowth, but I do it anyway. As soon as I'm holding her in my arms something shifts inside. The feel of her tiny body, her birth-reddened cheek against my skin does feel like a miracle. When I look at Mum all I see is sunshine pouring out of her, bathing us in happiness.

There are photos of me at this moment and my eyes look like they're taking up half my face. I am hypnotized by new life.

Dad slings his arm round my shoulder. "You'll take care of her with us."

I nod, knocked speechless by the waves of emotions surging through me, still feeling the zing of Orla's kiss on my lips.

Her name, Mum says, is Sula. Dad's springing around the place. "It means peace and 'Little She Bear!'" He laughs. That makes me and Orla laugh because she's as hairy as a bear!

Our home is love, laughter, tiredness and brightness. If Orla could I think she would move in but as they leave the flat I hear her mum say, "We must leave them to bond now. It's family time."

Time in days and hours melts into another phase. Sula has brought her own strange clock. Like the rest of the world has faded away and it's just me, Mum, Dad and Sula in our little nest … and Orla upstairs, her kiss still printed on my lips.

Strange how I have no memory of school at that time. I went. I didn't want to but I showed up and tried to concentrate…

Dad cooks, cleans and plays the sweetest music I've ever heard from him. Mum's always sleeping, feeding, bathing, changing or rocking Sula. When Mum has a bath I hold Sula and watch her face *like sky-watching,* tracking every passing cloud that crosses. When she wakes and opens her eyes, staring into mine, her mouth lifts into a smile. Mum says it's only wind … but I see the shine in her eye and I know she's smiling at me. It feels like I'm holding the most precious being in the world in my arms, and the way she gazes back, unblinking, it seems she thinks I'm precious too.

Two weekends go by. Orla and her mum are coming over. I've hardly seen Orla in school and my heart is pounding with nerves like I'm about to meet a stranger. I open the door and Orla blushes like she's embarrassed to see me too. She brings Sula a present – a yellow blanket she's knitted herself. Mum wraps her in it and lets Orla hold her close. Tears of joy are in Orla's eyes and I want to kiss her now, right here in front of everyone. I want to run out on the balcony and shout to the world that I am Kai, and this is the best day of my life – I have my family and Orla to love.

"Did I see a little look between you and Orla?" Dad teases later as I hold Sula. "Do I need to have that talk with you?" He nudges me, making me squirm. Why does he always have to be so out there?

"Get a filter!" I want to say, but I think I'm a bit like Dad that way. I don't think I've got much of a filter either.

Dad picks up one of the 'New Baby!' congratulations cards and laughs. "So you know Sula wasn't carried in by a stork then?"

"Dad! It's not like that." I sigh, but in a way I'm happy that he's starting to notice I'm not a kid any more.

Dad tiptoes over to the bedroom to check on Mum. "Sleeping peacefully!" he reports, touching his finger to his lips, pointing from sleeping Sula to Mum. Placing an arm round my shoulder, I can hear his heart beat slow and strong.

Like I said ... it was the time of bliss.

All I can feel is this ache of happiness in my heart.
And all the foreshadowings –
the fallen chick,
Dad's rant in the Tower,
unbalanced wings –
have flown far, far away and everything is golden.

Ever since Orla kissed me I've been wondering if I should ask her out, if she's been waiting for me to. Now seems like a good moment as we walk down to the Bothy together for the first time since Sula was born. I take a deep breath and I'm just about to ask when she links arms.

We are standing in the archway, all that's left of our old den. *She's right: this is a good place…*

It's just so embarrassing. How to reach across this in-between space? I hesitate.

"Kai, can we keep that kiss a secret?" Orla whispers.

"Why?" I step back to look at her.

"I don't know. It's a bit like how you felt about our secret sunshine handprints. It might ruin things with the three of us. I don't think I'm ready for any of this. I was so happy for you. We should all just be friends."

"Sure." I shrug and try to make my voice light.

How did I feel then, though I said nothing at all? I felt as if my heart were breaking. Just for a moment in our nest at home, holding Sula, dreaming of kissing Orla again, everything had been perfect.

Zak brings a present of a teddy bear for baby Sula from his parents. Dad's told everyone she's our 'little bear' and now that's all people get her! As he hands it to me he says he's overheard his mum and dad talking about trying for another baby.

"Wouldn't that be brilliant? They could be friends like us!" Orla springs a hug on him and starts on about how she could be a sister to his baby too. And I make the right noises of being happy at that idea but what I'm thinking as I lean against our secret sunshine handprints is, *I hope it doesn't happen. Why do your family have to have everything we've got and more? Can't you let us have our moment?* What I would like to do is kiss Orla right now in front of Zak, just to show him that me and Orla have something more, but I stay quiet, seething inside, watching it all unfold.

I'm not proud of myself. I never whisper a word about this resentment towards Zak that's been growing in me and, no matter how much I'm tempted to, I never break my promise and speak to Zak about kissing Orla.

But sometimes you don't have to say things for people to feel what's in the silence. I've learned that much. These days our secrets hang around the Bothy walls, just flaking paint away from being discovered.

So, even though me and Orla never kiss again, nothing is the same.

Like most days after school, me and Zak find our way to the Bothy. Orla makes some excuse that she has to go straight home. No matter what she says about having too much on or being behind with her homework, I know she's avoiding me.

To fill the silences Zak's brought a dartboard that belonged to his dad. He was going to throw it out because of health and safety so Zak thought he'd bring it here for us. "Dad doesn't need to know!" he says. They're the sort of darts that actually make holes instead of the magnet ones that ricochet back off. I like the way they bury deep into the pockmarked wood. Every match you have is somehow recorded there for all time.

I'm poised, aiming for the bullseye. I miss three times and go to retrieve my darts, having to twist and turn to work them out of the board again.

"You don't have to throw so hard!" Zak says.

"My eye's out anyway." I shrug. "Can't concentrate! We don't get much sleep with the baby."

"I can hear Sula crying from here!" Zak listens out for a moment as he takes aim and only just misses...

"Dad says she's got opera singer's lungs," I tell him as this time he hits his mark.

"Bullseye!" he shouts, jabbing the air.

And suddenly I want to pick up a dart and plant it in his back. My friend from the first day of primary. My friend who I stood with, stark naked, in the middle of winter. Skinny kids blowing a giant wishing bubble over Greenlands. Why do I feel this rage inside every time I think of him or see him? Maybe because he's turning out to be the golden boy, his blazer covered in achievement badges, when no one seems to notice me or if they do it's only Salter raising an eyebrow, spreading doubts about me among the other teachers... Even Zak's mum calls me in to have a little "check-in chat" with her. Maybe it's the easy way Zak has of talking to teachers or anyone. Or maybe it's because deep down I think Zak is the reason why Orla doesn't want to kiss me again.

"Remember when you came back to mine, that first time, and we blew that giant bubble over Greenlands? I wished for Sula. What did you wish?" I ask him as he aims at the board.

Zak laughs. "Random! What makes you think of that now?" he asks, pulling his darts out of the board, offering them to me. I shrug and shake my head. He elbows me... The old sign to start sparring.

He drops the darts and grabs me round the shoulders. We wrestle each other to the ground, pushing and pulling like how we used to rough-tumble over each other when we were kids. But mid-tussle, before I know it, I've got him in a lock, twisting his arm, jabbing his elbow upwards.

"Time! Kai!" he shouts and I shove his arm a bit higher before I get a hold of myself and loosen my grip. "What's got into you?" He pushes me away and stands up, rubbing his arm where I yanked it. I say nothing.

"Maybe you've got issues like your dad."

I want to aim a dart into his eye. "Why do you say that?" I ask, backing away, afraid of what I'll do if I'm too close to him.

"Sorry. Something Orla said. I love your dad..."

"But you were talking about him behind my back, right?" I snap back.

Zak frowns and shakes his head. He picks up his bag

and looks round the Bothy, grabbing the darts like he doesn't trust me with them. "You wanted to know what I wished back then...?" He shoves past me as he bashes open the Bothy door, turning to spit this out. "That you and me would be friends forever... Brothers." With that he kicks the rotten wood against the hinges with a deafening crack.

I cried like a baby after that and I wanted more than anything to call Zak and tell him I was sorry. But, every time I picked up the phone to talk to him, this fire licked at my throat because of what I overheard Dad say one day that stuck in my head. "That Zak's got it all going on for him. He'll go far." Like he saw something in Zak that I didn't have... Everyone else always said that me and Zak were so alike we could be brothers, but Dad seemed to know different. I think that's why I wanted to hurt Zak because I couldn't shed the feeling that whatever and whoever I was, he would always be more... Even Dad knew it.

And now?

Left behind, sitting on this Green Hill, from the outside it would seem like that were true, but the rage has burned itself out. Instead of the pain I felt that day, all I can hear is the sweetness of Zak's wish for us when we were skinny little kids and the rest was still to come. What I can't believe is how he's stuck by me all this time; after everything I threw at him he never let me push him away.

I give it ages before I go back home after the bust-up with Zak, but Mum sees my eyes are swollen from crying and she's not going to let it go so I tell her about the fight. Not what it was about though. I want to ask her what I should do. How to make it right with Zak but, while I'm talking, she's drifting off to sleep, feeding Sula.

The next day I make sure I'm late up so Orla doesn't wait for me on the way into school.

"Best go on!" Dad says, when he opens the door to her. "You don't want sleepyhead to make you late!"

At lunch break I try to keep out of the way so I don't bump into Zak in the quad. But it's no good. There he is, sitting on a table with a crowd of others I don't know.

He tries to catch my eye, but I turn away. Best to steer clear of each other.

Just my luck that I pass Zak's mum in the corridor, hurrying to a class, but she still stops and asks after my mum and the new baby. "Doesn't seem long since you and Zak were babes in arms!" She shifts around a bit, as if I'm making her uncomfortable, and I realize I'm checking out her belly for signs.

What am I supposed to say! "Yeah, Mum's fine and Sula too," I tell her. I wish she wouldn't talk to me in front of everyone.

"Great, and Kai, straighten your tie!" She points at my slack knot. I do. At least Zak hasn't told her about our scrap.

On Friday, when Orla comes down to our flat to see Sula, she keeps asking me why I'm being so quiet. I say "no reason", but what I want to say is, "because you've been talking about my dad to Zak and you've got no business to. So why should I trust you?"

Zak hasn't been back to the Bothy all week and I don't ask him to. Orla shows up less and less. It's just too awkward between all of us.

When Dad asks why the three of us don't hang out any

more I shrug and say, "We're in different friendship groups."

Dad pats me on the back. "Well, do you want to talk about it?"

I shake my head but he doesn't let it go. "I had a really hard time of it at your age. Three different foster carers and three different schools in the first few years of secondary. You get to stay in the same place with your mates, instead of always being handed on. Stick with your friends, Kai... They'll see you right. Don't go getting into the wrong crowd, like I did." With every word Dad's forehead furrows deeper like between these words he's remembering so much more than he's saying. "Whatever's gone on between you, make it up with them. I always thought you three musketeers would be friends forever!"

"In case you hadn't noticed, we're not kids any more, Dad!" I groan as he grabs me by the shoulders and hugs me to him hard.

"You're still my first-born baby!" I shrug him off and pull away because I'm ashamed of what I think that day.

I wish I could tell you that you were the reason we argued. You were the reason I fought with Zak. It's your fault. I don't want you ever to get weird like you did that day at the Tower again. Just stay like this from now on – hold steady for all our sakes.

Weeks slide by in Sula time, feeding, nappy changing, watching her sleep. Dad's steady as a rock right now, but not me. I don't even worry about the ravens that have taken to trailing me to my balcony door. I've got used to the miracle of Sula being here and I can't wait till she can toddle around and speak. I just want to know who she's going to be. Mum says my sister has a feisty little personality but I don't see how she can tell that!

Now that Zak isn't around any more and it's all awkward with Orla, Dad's taken to coming down to the Bothy with me because I think he can feel I need him here. Odd though it is for us to be there together, I like it. If I could I'd fly back in time to when it was just Dad and me on Greenlands, wilderness warriors cutting through.

We are "song-weaving" together. Dad has a go at teaching me the sax again and, instead of complaining about practising like I used to, I let him teach me and actually find my way to some of the old tunes.

"I always said you've got my ear, Kai. I love teaching you… If you want me to."

"Maybe," I say.

But I know what Dad's doing, hanging out down here, trying to get me to open up a bit about my friends.

I don't really tell him anything, but he's happy again, like he trusts that everything's going to be OK. I love my dad so much for knowing that I need him now in the place we have always been closest, our Greenlands clearing.

We hang out in the Bothy for ages, hardly noticing the time slipping by until we hear Mum's voice calling. Dad checks his pocket. "I should have brought my phone. I promised Mum I'd cook."

Such ordinary, unremarkable words.

Dad sets off at a jog out of the Bothy and up the hill, the ravens screeching above us. I turn it into a race and despite his head start I catch up with him at the top.

Mum's standing on the balcony, smiling and waving at us... I think.

Hard smiling, hard waving, cradling Sula to her.

Dad's picking up pace, slamming through the metal door. "What's the hurry?" I rush after him, raven wings shadowing the dappled paths. *Mum is smiling, isn't she?*

No, not a smile. Mum's mouth is open wide. Skin pulled tight in pain. I watch her turn, take someone's hand and go inside.

Time slows.

Dad's shrieking, "Jan, Jan, what's going on?" His feet are

pounding the path now, so I lag behind.

If only we had steps to climb to her like I've always wished for.
I hear the bang of the metal door, the slam.
I smell the bitter stench of sweat as I follow Dad inside to find
Holly, Orla's mum,
leaning over Sula
lying in her yellow blanket on the sofa.
Hands on her tiny chest.
Mouth over her mouth.
I am frozen.
I am nothing but a beating heart,
watching flying limbs.
Mum's arms beating at Dad's chest,
blame raging through her.
"Where were you, Dexter?"
Orla's crouched up in the corner,
crying and crying.
Ravens swooping, screeching.
"Kai, close your balcony window,"
Dad orders,
Beating wings, wanting in.
I slide the doors closed.
Slump on my bed,
pull my duvet over my head and hide.

From here I am
outside or inside myself, I can't tell.
A blue light flashes;
inside Mum howls.
Orla's hands are over her mouth.
My heart is a punching, pummelling, pounding drum.
I close my eyes against its rhythm
but all I can hear is the screech of ravens and all I can see
is the twisted, lifeless chick
and the pale blue of sky cracked open.

Holly and Orla are out on the balcony.
Wrapped in my duvet I stumble out.
We stand together
to see Mum and Dad climbing into the ambulance.
The siren sounds sharp in the crisp night air.
Shadows of raven wings swoop through the trees.

Why won't Orla's mum say anything?
Holly's eyes are red-rimmed with tears.
Her hands clasped tight over her mouth.
After a while words splutter out.
"I tried, Kai, to get her breathing again. I tried, I tried."

Sounds blocked out.
Holly is moving her mouth,
speaking to me.
Orla is moving her mouth,
speaking to me.
No shine in our eyes only
tears and tears
and tears.

Shivering, Orla lifts my arm
so she can step inside the duvet too.
She brings no warmth,
buries her head in my chest.
I am frozen.
Heart pounding
through skin
and I hate myself.
I wish it would stop beating
so Sula's could start again
and I would be as cold as death.
Not her.

Hovering on the threshold,
the ravens hop off the railings to the balcony floor,
demanding to know more.

It's my idea to plant a tree for Sula on my birthday, six months after we lost her. It feels like the right time to me but Mum says we should have it on another day. "Your birthday is yours, Kai, and something we'll always celebrate." We can't though. Who wants to celebrate my birthday now Sula's dead? Not me. I figure planting a memorial tree in Greenlands wood could be good for all of us and I thought doing something together, digging in the earth, might help.

We're supposed to go to the garden centre to choose it but in the end, after waiting ages for him, Dad doesn't even come out of the bedroom. Mum says, "Let's go. Your dad's not up to it today. He's happy for us to choose."

But Mum's not happy and I'm not either. I want to bash down their bedroom door, drag Dad out and scream at him. *Just do this for me and Mum!*

Mum's lips are drawn tight but she doesn't say anything. I feel so sorry for her having to hold everything together because Dad can't.

At the garden centre we stand among the rows of trees, arms hanging at our sides, just staring at them. How can we decide which one should be for Sula? A tall man with white hair and smile wrinkles around his eyes comes over and asks if he can be of any help. I want to laugh because I feel like screaming to the sky, YES PLEASE. WE NEED

EVERY KIND OF HELP.

But Mum smiles back politely, zipping herself in, as she explains to the man that what we're looking for is a memorial tree. He asks a lot of technical questions about where we're planning to plant it and, after thinking for a while, he says, "An evergreen would be nice because it can be visited all year round. I favour the eucalyptus for its silvery leaves. Some people think they look a bit like tears, but they're more heart-shaped to my mind."

We want a big one but when we look at the price tag we can't believe how expensive they are so we go for the one Mum thinks we can just about afford, which is the smallest. The tree man gives us a ticket and tells us to pay at the front desk and he'll take it round the back for us to collect.

After we've paid we meet the tree man in the car park and hand him our receipt.

"Where's your car?" he asks. "I'll load it up."

"Don't have one. We walked," Mum explains.

Tree Man nods and lifts up the eucalyptus, much bigger than the spindly one we chose. He winks at me. "You look like a strong boy – you up to carrying this?"

I nod, wishing Dad were here with us.

"Lay it over your back, son… Spread the weight evenly, that's right."

I balance it over my shoulder like a broken wing and with every step it grows heavier. Now Sula's funeral seems like yesterday and I feel as if I'm carrying my sister's coffin home. I know Mum's crying. I hold my back proud and straight so she won't know tears are streaming down my face too.

By the time we're at Greenlands, my neck and back are aching so much they burn, but not as much as the ache in my chest that feels like it's about to split open.

Walking down the hill, me and Orla carry the tree between us and I think about how Mum didn't even try that hard to rally Dad to come. I wonder if she's thinking what I am, that if he does manage to play his sax it will be like a little miracle.

"What'll you play for Little Bear, Dex?" Mum asked before we left, smoothing over his crumpled shirt. These days she treats him like *he's* the baby.

"'Somewhere Over the Rainbow'. Sula's song."

Mum held Dad for a long time and I wanted to squeeze between them like I used to, but I'm nearly as tall as Mum now and anyway, since Sula died, we don't fit together the way we used to.

Orla stands by my side and Holly by Mum's. I feel Dad's shadow-self behind us, hardly there at all. This is what I think as I take the spade and dig at the earth in the exact place where I buried the fallen chick. No sign of blue-sky fragments now. Mum says no speeches are needed, so all there is left to do is to place Sula's tree in the hole we've dug.

Maybe Dad wouldn't come down here because he doesn't want to spoil all our old memories. Maybe I think that too as I turn round to see if he'll play the sax like he said he would. Our balcony door's open but he's not there.

As Orla pours the water in and I pat the ground around the roots Holly makes a strange rasping sound. She says it's keening not crying. It sounds deeper than crying. She talks to Mum a lot about grief. How everyone thinks being a midwife is the best job in the world and it is until it's the worst. She tells us now, through her tears that she says are for Sula, but also for others she carries in her heart. I know it makes Mum feel better that she's not on her own. It helps her to go to the group that Holly told her about but I wish everyone would stop talking now. *Not-talking* and standing here, all of us together, planting Sula's tree, is what would have helped me.

Holly's going on now, afraid of silence settling, telling Mum that in some places in the world there are professional mourners who start off the crying, like they can draw on this well of tears and help other people to cry too. Mum smiles but behind her eyes I can't tell what she's thinking. Maybe Holly's stories do help Mum. If I could find a way to help Dad keen or even just cry I would.

As we place the tree into the ground I hear a weak squeaking sound from behind. Everyone looks up to our balcony where Dad stands, holding his sax, ready to play. His tall, gaunt figure casting shadows over our wood where on this first day of September the leaves are already curling into autumn.

In my mind I blow a giant wishing bubble and send it floating up to Dad, willing him to play his sax again. *Go on, Dad … play. Please play for Sula, for me and Mum too.*

I hear the notes of 'Somewhere Over the Rainbow', the first song he tried to teach me. He says it's Sula's song because he used to play it to her. Maybe he's forgotten it was our song too. Somewhere inside I feel that if Dad could play today then everything would change. If we could only have our music back. I close my eyes. Orla reaches for my hand and I wait and wait and wish as hard for this as I once wished for Sula.

But only a single tortured note tears out of him.

One long, ugly-sounding broken cry.

He tries again and again
and I know
in that moment
that Dad's breath as well as his heart is broken.

That's when I notice movement in the flat above Orla's. A woman and a boy bow their heads as if they're listening to Dad too. I want to yell at them, "What are you staring at? This has nothing to do with strangers!"

The woman's shaking her head and trying to persuade the boy to move inside, as if she senses this is our private ceremony. Not for them to see. I wish everyone would leave us to howl at the sky, to face this ourselves. Just me and Mum and Dad. Right now I wish even Orla and Holly would go away and let us be... Just us three. I bend down to find a tiny piece of egg poking through the soil and pick it up. I haven't heard a song thrush for so long. Perhaps they've gone from here, taking their blue sky with them. I crush the tiny shard of shell to powder in my hands. That's what we are – the crushed shells of ourselves. And, no matter how much Mum tries to put on a brave face, if anyone didn't know how sad we are they do now Dad's blasted out his hopeless note for everyone to hear.

I never truly understood how a tragedy plays out,
but now I do. Tragedy doesn't make you big but
shrunken, shattered and small. Tragedy is when all
you love is music and there's nothing left in you to
play. Tragedy is the death of hope. Tragedy is us,
standing on this Green Hill, planting our pain in
Greenlands.

Without Dad by my side Mum steps in to hold me. "It's OK, try to talk, let the feelings out," she says, but all I can see when I look into her eyes is the sadness that sweet Sula is not in her arms. That I cannot be Sula, that I will never be Sula. I know that every time she holds me she will ache with sadness that I am not her baby.

"It's nobody's fault, Kai. We didn't know she had a faltering heart." Mum keeps telling me the same thing but she doesn't understand about low heavens or broken skies. I haven't told anyone that right here, where we planted Sula's tree, I buried the shrivelled song thrush. I should have warned them.

I'm starting to feel deep in me that this is my fault, because *if* I'd warned them they might have had Sula checked out. If they had she could still be alive now…

Mum doesn't know, and not even Orla can know because she talks to Zak and I'm not having him and his family interfering in our business. Nobody knows except for the ravens and me. Maybe that's why they flew up to our flat on the day she was born… To warn me. And I didn't listen, did I?

Every day that passes I feel it more. This is all my fault. I should have heard the ravens' call… Mum doesn't understand that these ravens that stand by Sula's tree today want to be our friends, that they tried to warn us. She and Holly shouldn't keep shooing them away, going on about their mess. They have to stop trying to unbalance their wings. Only me and Dad get this.

But it's Mum, not Dad, who walks with me to Sula's tree every day before school. Dad watches from the balcony in his pyjamas and just about manages to lift his hand to wave.

"Got your kit for the match?" Mum asks.

"I don't feel like playing footie today."

Mum tries a cheery voice. It just sounds wrong and she's biting her lip, not sure she should say what she's about to. "Guess what! Zak's dad called on the off chance. He can't make your game today … he asked if Dad fancied stepping in as coach! Says it's all getting a bit much for him as he's got a lot of work on. So I'll see what he says. Maybe you'll catch up with your dad later on at the Rec."

The bit of me that can still let wish bubbles float through my mind lights up. Perhaps this will help to get Dad through. But then I hear Dad's night crying in my head, casting doubt on my hope.

Is he up to it? Is that a good idea? I don't question because I see the tears pooling at the rims of Mum's eyes. She dams them in but I know how hard she has to try to get Dad to do anything these days. So I switch out of my worries, put on a brave face like she does and say, "Right! Well, if he's coach count me in."

What happened to time after we planted Sula's tree? I don't know but things slid fast and faster. I can't remember at what point Dad's compassionate leave ended and he was let go from his nightshift. "Let go." Mum always talked like that. Sacked or made redundant, she meant. Nothing compassionate about that.

We'd been doing what Holly later called "going through the motions". Waking, school, eating, sleeping… Well, the sleeping less and less. I've grafted together these times in my mind but somehow it was that last match I played on the Rec that made me see that the tragedy of Sula dying would not go away. And I think to protect myself after that day I finally followed in Dad's footsteps and stopped hoping for happiness.

Ever since Sula's dying day I could feel it in an abstract way, the shadows falling, ready to engulf the sky and swallow us whole, but it was not until the day of the match that I saw how unbalanced Dad's wings were. It wasn't properly scored into my heart until we were both coated in Greenlands mud and blood that I really understood how deep we had crawled into the undergrowth and entered the shadowlands.

For a while after Sula died even Salter attempted to crack a sympathetic smile, but as time goes by it's like whatever long leash they had me on is getting shorter. In class today Salter's back to his old ways, jabbing me with questions when he knows I've tuned out. I can't help it because the only thing on my mind is how I can head Dad off from coaching us later. The more I think about it the more I know it's a terrible idea. I should have told Mum not to persuade him into it. I should know by now to go with my gut.

At lunch break I keep trying to message Mum but get no answer so I call Dad instead, not expecting him to pick up but here he is.

"Dexter speaking!" His voice sounds brighter than it has in ages.

Starving hope surges in me. "Hi, Dad. You're awake!"

"Awake and ready for action! I'll see you after school on the Rec. You know what, son, it's been too long! I'm actually looking forward to it. No arguing with Coach!" he jokes. "It'll be like the old days."

I think, *Please don't go over the top, Dad,* but I try to sound as keen as him.

"See you later then."

I'm wiping the tears of happiness from my eyes as the siren sounds for end of lunch. "Haven't they changed that torture bell?" Dad says and I can hear the tension in his voice. "Get yourself to class then and stay out of Salter's way!" He hangs up on me before I have the chance to check again if he's really feeling OK.

At least it's art this afternoon. Usually I can let my mind wander but no chance of that because now I see the small, baby-shaped mound of Zak's mum's growing belly that no one's even told me about. Not Zak or Orla. So this is why they've been steering clear of me. She sees me looking and I know she's only being kind telling me my work's "improved no end", got "real depth", but I can't stand to have her anywhere near me, thinking of what's alive and somersaulting in her belly. Zak's baby brother or … sister.

And I start hating on Zak some more. I wish his mum wouldn't come so near me with her kind eyes and her baby belly, her questions and chatting on – like she gives a toss if Dad's coaching the match later on. Then it dawns on me. I wonder if Dad stepping in is their interfering way of checking out how we're doing, spying on us or maybe … pity. If Orla talks to Zak about us then why wouldn't Zak talk to his mum and dad too? Shame neither of them could pluck up the courage to tell me about the baby. I can't trust anyone.

Changing into my kit, I feel like saying I'm sick. I wish they'd all leave us alone and stick their noses out of our business. How can any of them understand?

When we're out on the pitch, kicking around, my nerves about Dad turn to anger. The other team have already arrived in their brand-new bus. *Where is Dad?* People keep looking over like him being late is down to me. The other team's already warming up with their coach but still no sign of Dad – maybe him not showing up is the best thing that can happen now.

"Is your coach coming then?" the other coach asks

as I retrieve our ball from the sidelines. I've seen him before – he's a grit-for-voice shouter. Always down on us. He's probably hoping Dad won't show up too.

"Yeah!" I say, pretending to concentrate on counting toe kicks when I hear Mum call over and wish I could bury myself under Sula's tree.

I did wish that. More than once. That's how it felt at that time, like I wanted to curl up into a shell and lie with her in the earth. But no one knew…

Mum's walking ahead of Dad, rallying him on like a kid who doesn't want to play, and then I see him. He's made a bit of an effort but I can already tell by the hang of his shoulders that he's changed his mind and he's not up to this.

"I'd just about given up on you! It's a bit rich us battling our way through the traffic, getting here on time… I thought you were local," the other coach complains, eyeing dad suspiciously. But all the same he offers him his hand to shake and says his name is Rory.

"Yeah. I'm coach today." Dad peers over at the posh school bus they arrived in, a luxury coach compared to our beaten-up old van.

He doesn't shake Rory's hand or introduce himself.

Instead he eyes him back like he wants to plant his fist into his face. Especially when Rory says, "I just think we need to set an example. If we're going to ask the teams to show up on time...'

I dribble the ball away to where Mum's watching so I don't have to hear Dad's answer but as Rory walks away I catch Dad giving him the finger. I know Mum's seen it too but she's pasted that fixed mask smile on her face. "You shouldn't have brought him. It's obvious he's not OK," I say through clenched teeth and boot the ball away.

Dad's all hang-head and cursing under his breath as he calls us into a huddle for our team talk, but instead of rallying us he says, "Right, boys, let's show that entitled tosser what we're made of!"

Some of the lads laugh, awkward laughter, stoking themselves up, but I've checked the light of caution in Zak's eyes. He sees me seeing. We know each other too well to hide. Today, crushed up close together, it strikes me how alike we look, except he's still wearing his healthy glow from visiting his family in St Lucia again. It's like the sun's under his skin even on this grey day.

"So much in common," our families used to say, because Dad's birth parents came from the Caribbean too, though we don't know which island. Dad going on about being "entitled" rings in my ears now as I face Zak We've never even been to the place our family came from. Can't even dream of it.

Zak slings his arm round me in a comradely gesture. I elbow him out of the way. "When were you going to tell me about your mum?" I mumble it but he hears OK.

"Kai, I..."

He reaches for me again, but I turn away. Me and Zak might have been brothers once but we've got nothing in common any more.

"What about our warm-up?" I ask Dad.

He yawns and shakes his head. "How about you and Zak take charge?"

I guide Dad away from the team and try to remind him he's supposed to be our coach but I don't think he hears me. He doesn't even greet the other parents from our team, come to support. Hardly any from Greenlands, mostly from Zak's side of the Rec. One woman makes a point of coming over and I hear her say, "Dexter, good to see you out and about. We're so sorry for your loss." And he bends his head low and strides away without uttering a single word. He doesn't even stand beside Mum.

The parents huddle together, closer now. I feel the fist of humiliation twist in my gut and I just want to protect Dad from this. *Are they talking about him? Wondering what's going on?* I can see it in their eyes – they suspect he's not up to it either.

Then, just when I think things can't get any worse, I catch sight of Zak's mum walking out of school towards us. "Hi, Faith!" Mum calls as she smiles and waves her over. Weird how my brain switches to back when we were little at the sound of her name; as soon as she's out of Ravenscroft I can never think of her as a teacher. I suppose because before that she was Zak's mum.

She's wearing her coat so maybe Mum won't see … but as she draws closer I watch Mum hesitate as she clocks the bump, and twists her face back into a smile anyway. She straightens up, mask smile widening, and half raises her hand. *How can she stand this?* I kick the ball to the other end of the pitch and sprint after it. The ravens glide and screech above my head. I don't ignore them any more. They get how I feel better than anyone.

"Good to see you, Faith!" Mum greets her first – always putting on a brave face.

When I dig myself out of my thoughts I see them standing together. Faith with her belly full of life while Mum's as thin as the tree that we planted for Sula.

Just don't let Dad notice, don't let him see. He jogs over and warning words slip out of me. "You've got to do this right, Dad! For me and Mum and Sula." I know I've crossed the line as soon as I say her name because Dad freezes, his eyes sparking feverishly.

The ravens wheel round us, cawing. Spectator whisperings grow impatient.

My kneecaps are frozen and our dragon breath hangs in the air but I am so full up with foreshadowings I think my breath might flare as fire.

Zak runs over, rallying, reassuring. "We can handle this game together, for your dad."

I grab him by his shirt. "We don't need your pity. Was Dad being coach your idea?"

I see it in his eyes – it was.

Zak doesn't answer either way as the someone blows the whistle and we're in play.

Blood rushing through me,
blasting thought away.
I'm just feet and arms and legs and lungs.
We're all flat out.
Zak setting himself up,
dodging his shadow defender,
free of him now.
He raises his hand
but can't understand
why I won't pass to him.
"Pass, Kai, pass!"
he yells,

looking for Coach
hanging out on the sidelines
to back up his call.

Dad stands there
in silence.
A broken shell
while Grit-Voice roars,
takes over,
barks orders.
"Mark him!"
"Tackle him!"
"Bring him down!"
I hate him.
Maybe I can give Dad this one thing...
Switch.
Maybe I can make him forget for one moment...
Switch.
Switch.

      This is mine,
      this time it's mine.
            Leg it up the pitch,
            be the hero of the match.
Line up the ball,
balance.

Shine in my
eye,
      flash of a wing
      flying,
          steady,
          hold,
              lining up to score.

                    I see him too late
            glint from the corner of my eye,
       boot tackling too high.
"Foul!" I call before contact's made,
     boot meets skin on the side of my head.
          Blood gushes out,
              I'm bowed down,
              cupping the blood from my temples,
              feet running,
                  crowding me out.

Grit-Voice wades in now, pointing at me.
"The tackle was good. What was he doing out of position anyway?"

            I catch sight of Dad's face
              wild with anger,
              wild with grief.

Zak's wiping my face, helping me up. "Come on, man. Let's get you cleaned up." He's got my hand, pulling me away from the pitch where Mum and Faith are already waiting with the first-aid kit.

"Penalty!" I hear Dad shout.

"Might have known he was *your* son!"

There is blood in my eye, gushing down my forehead.

Let me crawl under with Sula.

I'm on the floor again with Mum gently cleaning the wound.

Shooing away the ravens.

"Shall I call for help?" Zak's mum asks.

"I think he'll be OK, Faith," Mum says. "It's bleeding a lot but seems superficial. He'll be fine, I think. I just won't let him sleep for a while when we're home."

"I never sleep anyway," I groan.

Superficial. That word seems wrong.

Why couldn't they see how hurt I was?
Nothing's superficial about what happens from now
on where I've lived for so long concussed, confused,
faint, floating, fading into shadow skin...

Grit-Voice's shout carries to me. "Aren't you even going to check if your own son's OK? I was told you used to be a professional player. What sort of coach are you?"

There's a scuffle around me,
shadow wings
battering my mind.
"Leave it, Dad! I'm all right!" I call,
but my head throbs to speak.
I watch it in slow motion.
Dad's arm pulling back,
arcing through the air,
taking a swing
in front of everyone.
Skin against skin,
fist into face,
with all his force.

Others are on him, holding him back. Faith's got her teacher voice on, calling off the match. Leading our team away.

I shrug Zak off from helping me up. "This is your fault!" I spit at him. "Just mind your own business in future."

Through my bloodied eyes I see the hurt in his. "Go to hell then, Kai! All I ever do is try to help you!" He spits a glob of venom and strides away.

Faith tells everyone to calm it down and disperse but Grit-Voice is still banging on about calling the police, about pressing charges for assault.

Now he's in the safe confines of his shiny bus, Faith's managing to talk him down. I watch her calming hand pressing all his hot air out, the other one resting on her belly.

I bet she's playing her ace card and telling him about our tragic family.

I see him lower his head and nod in our direction like he's sorry for the scene. He starts up the engine and drives away.

"Thank you, Faith. This is my fault. I shouldn't have persuaded him..." Mum starts, but she doesn't finish whatever she was going to say because Dad collapses in the mud in front of everyone, sobbing like his heart has been ripped out of him. Now everyone knows just how broken we are.

I forget my battered head and swelling eye and refuse all the offers of help. It feels like every step we take across the Rec the ground is about to open up and swallow us. Outside I am blooded and bruised; inside I am fire and flame. Mum tries to rally us, mumbling something about "her wounded soldiers".

It makes me sick all her talk of breathing deep and

brighter days to come, her constant pretending we can live in some sweet story again. I take Dad's arm and walk him back across the Rec to Greenlands. The ravens fly ahead of us, screeching. Fire in their wings. Fire in their eyes.

Dad is stony silent but his voice booms through my mind.

"Look to the shine in their eye, Kai." Those words over and over, chiming through me.

I'm looking. I see it now, Dad. I feel it.

That same day Mum takes Dad to see the doctor. Afterwards she explains that he's depressed and needs medical help. "I've got Holly and you have Orla and Zak to talk to but Dad's kept everything dammed up inside him," she explains.

I don't tell her, "I don't talk to anyone, not even you, and no one tells me anything." She doesn't need me cracking up.

Then she throws it in, casually. "Faith's taking a little time off but she's organizing some counselling for you at school, and if you want Orla and Zak can go too. We all need a bit of extra help through this."

I tell her no, that wouldn't help at all, talking to a stranger.

Whatever she's said to Mum, I don't think Faith taking maternity leave early has anything to do with "needing more rest". I reckon she feels guilty every time she sees me and that's why she's so set on introducing me to the grief counsellor in school who'll be "there for me" every Friday. What good's that? What about all the other days? It feels like I'm being handed over. When I finally meet her the counsellor smiles at me and says if I don't want to come on my own, or with friends who know what I've been through, perhaps our whole family could come together. That's what she suggests, "our whole family", and with those three words I decide I won't ever talk to her again.

Anyway, school's the only place I don't have to think about Sula.

But that doesn't stop me seething inside all the time.

Mostly people leave me alone now, especially Zak and Orla. Suits me – I don't want anything to do with them either.

But when I see them together, their arms wrapped round each other, that's all it takes.

Zak, my so-like-me-we-could-be-brothers – except you have everything and I have nothing. That's how it felt when I watched you two together in the quad that day.

Zak and Orla
close
closer
face to face
lips moving
eyes locked
smiling
leaning in
not much sunlight between you
closer and closer.

Heart and feet pounding concrete
pushing through.
Pulling away when you see me coming.
"All right, Kai?" you say, all innocent.
Blood flushes through me
fire flares inside
arms wheel
fists clench
body blow
propelled.

Orla's voice
screeching
crying

screaming
pleading me to stop
pummelling fists.

"Let him go, Kai. Let him go."
Blow after blow
he fights back.
Well matched,
pounding,
blood spattered
skin shattered
arm cracked.

"Back away, Kai, back away."

Restrained. Grabbing, pulling, grasping.
"Get your hands off me!"

Fading light in Orla's eyes.
Her cry in my ear.
Her face misted through my tears.
"Why, Kai, why?"

"Om, man. This is where concussion set in proper. This is where I'm not sure of the details any more. I can't take it any further for now. That's why I need to start handing it over... You got so much of what was going on."

"It's like that when you're new, on the outside ... you see everything!" Om's voice trembles with emotion.

I nod, laying down Om's art. Painting after painting of fires burning under the paths between Greenlands and school...

Between the Acts

Omid

You asked me to tell how I was looking at the situation from where our story began together, my brother. I tried to hold it in words but to write is still a big task for me, harder even than A-level study. I think the best way is to sit beside you and try to *speak* the truth of what I saw.

I must start with the first day we moved here.

I saw you, Kai – a tall boy-man, broad shoulders with coiled hair like my missing brother Ishy. The way you held your head low reminded me of him so much it hurt.

I saw that the women were in mourn-shroud emotion, the girl too, but it was the boy who walked with shadows, fire and ravens at his feet, who I looked to.

"This is perfect place for us," my aunt told me when we stood together on the balcony.

I could not think of perfect places but I understood she wished so hard for it. She closed her eyes, giving thanks, *Alhamdulillah*, that finally we were safe. As she prayed I looked over the small woodland to the school across the green field where in a few days I would go.

I read on my aunt's face that, despite the small flat and that we have no garden of our own, she was in a happy place for there is nothing in this world my aunt loves more than trees and wildlife. But you did not know then she is Doctor of Conservation – environmentalist – all you saw in us was strangers, refugees.

I knew this by your look on our first day here, like you did not welcome us.

"No, man. It wasn't like that," I interrupt.
Om holds his hand up as if to say, "It is my turn to speak."

I must tell what I witnessed. What I felt. People did not take us for who we are, did not see the potential in what we could be here in this country, and I had anger in my heart when you looked at me, but it made me stronger. I thought, *Let them learn who my Aunt Gisou is when her shadows lift and she has English language to show them. I too will show them.* These were my thoughts on the day I watched you and Orla and your mothers planting one small tree. The sight

of you brought shadow memories of my older brother Ishy and my mother and father too.

I asked Aunt Gisou about the tree and she looked closer, telling me it is eucalyptus. She explained, "Some believe if you burn a few leaves it will make everything pure again. The smell is fresh too, like new life.

"Let us leave them to their grieving, Omid," Aunt Gisou told me and so she went inside, but I stayed because, as a moth flies to a flame in the darkness, I saw you were like me and I could not turn away.

But then a sudden sound shrieked through the land. At first I was afraid it was my trauma shock screaming from somewhere inside and then I begin to understand it is some kind of music from within this new tower-home of Greenlands.

"Dad, trying to play his sax?"

"Yes, that I understood when I heard it again. Wailing notes played from some breath instrument the musician had no heart to play."

Aunt Gisou ordered me to go inside. "What strange

music is this?" she asked. "There is no joy in it. I wish it to stop."

We both wished the pain to stop with equal force, didn't we? Though then we did not know each other. This howl like a wounded beast released too many ghosts for us but knowing this pain was here also grew strange comfort in me. Like maybe, in time, these people can understand that tearing sound in me too and me and Aunt Gisou will one day plant ourselves into this land.

Sometimes I think we have travelled so long together my Aunt Gisou feels what is in my mind. "My nephew Omid... When we are settled here let us plant something too, a fig tree like in our orchard, if it is permitted."

When she rested I returned to the balcony and I watched you fall to the earth like my brother Ishy fell on his knees at the force of the blast. My legs shook, wanting to run to you. I thought, *I do not know where Ishy is, even if he is alive, but maybe I can save this boy who lives in this tower-home with me.* You see, Kai, you were always close to my brother in my heart.

In school I wore my shield of silence and no one crossed to me. Each day I looked for you but the tower was quiet, doors closed.

At weekends I looked out over this Greenlands again to a field next to school. I heard other students call it a "Rec", where they play football. Back then I wondered if I will ever have a friend again. Those first months in school I tried hard not to think of everyone who was gone… The forest of lost people I will need to plant.

Then one day through my stress my ears opened and I heard the whistle of a game, and my feet remembered football. The space of running, leaving thought behind. I thought this is something I can do and I decided to find a way to join this team.

But the sound of playing changed. In the distance I heard shouting like men in war.

Coming closer, I see by your father's shoulders, his collapsed chest, that it must be he who breaks bricks with his heart to make this Greenlands tower cry with his broken throat music.

Your family resembled people I have seen before walking on the road from despair. I thought, *If I can, if he lets me, I will show this boy I understand. I will try to help him.*

"Om, sometimes I wonder if I'd be here at all if you hadn't seen what was going on."

He shakes his head. "We helped each other, as brothers do, that is all."

I wanted to help. I looked for opportunities with football but time passed and your door was closed to me. Sometimes I felt we were all locked inside this tower.

Some months went by and I was standing in the playground after eating with Orla, because Zak's mother asked her to be my mentor. How did she say it...? "To make me comfortable in my own skin." I thought, *Miss, if you had seen what I have seen you too would not find comfort in your skin.*

It was Orla who first shortened my name to Om. I could not speak well in English to argue these things but I was not offended as I saw that she had kindness in her eyes. She was friendly and if she saw me alone she asked if I would like to walk and talk with her. Her mother too was friendly with Aunt Gisou.

"Sorry, Om. I don't even know where I was... I hardly noticed anything."

"I know, I know. It was a hard time to pass for both of us."

Before I knew it I was Om to everyone except Aunt Gisou. In my loneliness I studied hard and words began to come in English easier. And, as I learned, I understood much more than anyone saw. Sometimes I spoke to Orla and Zak. They were friendly but it was you I kept looking to. Maybe because I was searching for my true brother.

For the first months I was sitting separate in many classes. Learning quickly with translators' help. All the time at home, online, catching up in English language. Aunt Gisou teaching me science far advanced of anything we learned in school. My brain was sharpened every day.

At the gathering evening to show progress my Aunt Gisou smiled politely when the art teacher told her I was gifted, but she was only interested to speak to the science teacher. Even though Aunt Gisou's speaking was improving, her progress in English was much slower than mine. My science teacher said, "Om has a sharp brain; his grades are very high." This I understood and translated to my aunt.

"Omid, tell your teachers to call you by your true name and explain that our brains need to be sharp to withstand what we have survived." I did not want to cause any difficulty so I did not claim claim back my name. Instead I explained that my Aunt Gisou is a scientist and she teaches me well. My chemistry teacher sat forward in his seat. This is the strangest thing. When they hear the word refugee I don't know what they are imagining. That a woman like Aunt Gisou had no life before coming here, no career, like we were all born on the road from despair? That made me burn with anger inside but I only sat next to Aunt Gisou and smiled, as I have learned to do.

Outside of classes I decided I would be like the raven birds that fly over the wood and come to sit on railings of our tower. I could have taught you, if you had allowed me to be your friend at that time... There is power in watching first. There is power in silence. I saw it in these birds that have a look like survivors. I saw in their eyes that they, like me, understand more than you think. I told myself, be patient. I will watch and I will wait, until my speaking English is good enough so that everyone will see me as I am. In the between time, until my understanding and my speaking flow together as one, I decided I would paint what I saw. For in paint I need no translation.

"That's my first real memory of you, in the art room," I tell Om, picking up his portfolio.

Om nods. "You say you would not have survived without me, but I think neither you or I would survive without art."

"I wish I'd met you earlier. Maybe things..."

Om places his hand on my arm. "There is no point to think in a back-facing way. Trust me, I know."

There was fire in the air that day. I did not understand why, but I felt it.

Orla ran from my side across the quad, arms outstretched, hair floating behind her like waves. Now she started jumping up and down with joy. She was very happy, throwing her arms and legs round Zak. I looked away, embarrassed. I did not think before they were this kind of friend. Then in one moment, flashing across my eyes, I saw you, Kai. I backed away, making myself small as I have learned to do in battle, but I witnessed it all: the violence, the fire, the anger, the wish to cancel out the happiness of another.

The following day I observed that you did not attend school and also not for one whole week after. Orla told me it was because of your violence. Every day she was sad when we passed your door, and after she always looked to the small tree as we passed the Greenlands wood. One day I decided to ask Orla for some history of what happened to your family. I opened conversation by repeating what my aunt said – that planting eucalyptus is a sign of purifying, if you burn the leaves. But Orla cut my speech with sharp eyes and told me no one must ever harm this tree. I said she mistook my meaning and I tried to ask gently about the tree? But she would not answer me. Like to speak of you or it was to betray. This loyalty I understood, but it reminded me that I was the outsider, not trusted. After that I did not ask again.

Towards the end of Year Eight I finally grew the courage to try for the football team but did not find a place. Instead I poured my feeling into art and expression came out of me, like a river. In school I found a new home – the art room. I watched Zak and Orla grow close, bonded. Girlfriend and boyfriend.

"I can't believe I hardly even noticed you and you saw all this."

Om smiles sadly and just carries on.

In my ink paintings I thought of you at home. This family locked inside. After school and at night from my balcony I heard you play your music full volume, too high. Sometimes, in the wood, your dance with ravens made you wild. Hands, head, arms jerking this way, that way, backways arching, kicking off with feet and falling. Trying the same move over again. The music and dance were angry – hot, repeated beats, good for fighting, good for blasting all thought away. I understood.

Aunt Gisou grew troubled. She was saying she will complain about the noise. "First the father with his heartbreak music, now the son with this cacophony." She warned me, "Omid, keep away from this family and that raven boy." But she was also sorry for them. She told me then what she had learned from Orla's mother, the tragedy this family had faced.

Understanding of this, for me, changed everything. It was the first time I prayed in this country. I prayed for you and for me and for Ishy too. From the first day I saw you I felt some brother feeling but now I understood. I decided I could not stand by and watch the fires and shadows take you.

Later that day when Aunt Gisou rested I went out to this woodland. I walked past the young tree with silver leaves dancing and heard a sound from below my feet.

At first I thought it came from under the earth. I thought maybe Ishy was calling to me to save him as he does in my nightmares … trapped in the ground and waiting for me to pull him into life. Too late I let myself remember. I could not breathe but from the grey cloud above rain fell like a blessing. I tasted it on my tongue and it woke me back to where I stood. More sudden rain fell hard and the path became mud-clay. I was slipping down and falling in the direction of the cry. Raven birds swooped above me, wings shining, rainbow colours flashing. The note of heartache I could not ignore.

I came to the building and saw you, curled into a corner, making moaning sounds like a wounded dog.

"Zak? Orla?" you called. I pushed the door and you cowered from me. Your face covered in mud, mine too from my fall. We were like boys of clay made from the same earth even if I am from faraway soil. I forgot all my English words and in my panic I spoke to you in Arabic, remember?

I raised my hands to say do not fight me – you have nothing to fear from me. Finally words returned to me. "My name is Omid, but people here call me Om." I saw that you were in a space beyond words so I pointed to the balcony above, saying, "I live here too."

You nodded to me then like you knew but your mind was clouded. Your eyes were blood and fire. I felt in me, by instinct, that you and me were held inside the sadness of this globe. I was feeling sore in my heart for you. "Brother."

That is all I said and, even though you are bigger than me, taller, stronger, broad of shoulders, I walked inside the flake-paint yellow room and took you in my arms and rocked you like you were a baby, as my Aunt Gisou held others on the road from despair. You allowed me. I saw that my instinct on first sight of you when we moved here was true. Your need was great, and mine was too.

Sometimes you can feel what another feels in your blood flow, in the beating of your heart, and in your open arms. I also knew that, in this care for you, finally I have one friend. For my part it was a bond without the need of words.

When you became calm you did speak some words, and in the dance of your arms, the look in your eyes, I think I understood. "Please don't tell anyone about this… Secret place… Bothy." You placed your fingers over your mouth and shook your head.

"What is this *Bothy*?" I did not understand the word or the place we were inside. You did not answer. So I just said, "OK, it can be secret." Who will I tell?

After that we walked together past the tree I saw your family planting on our arrival day and you told me simply, "This tree we planted for my baby sister – her name was Sula."

My tears fell and in that moment I knew you trusted me with the deep of your heart, like brothers do.

On Monday I saw Orla leave early in her uniform. It was better for me that she had finally stopped asking if I wanted to walk with her. At the bottom of the steps I heard the door open and you were there in front of me. You straightened your tie and nodded, looking shameful, like you wanted to forget we met. So I did what I had planned to do – show you the photo of my brother Ishy.

From that day on, through the rest of Year Eight, then Years Nine and Ten, it was always Om and Kai. Aunt Gisou's heart was softened because she learned the tree was planted for a baby. We walked together every day and the raven birds walked with us. Sometimes you spoke more to the ravens than me but it did not matter. I had a brother. I was no longer alone.

For our GCSE exam art portfolio the teacher asked us to draw portraits of each other, of the person next to us. One lesson I sat and painted you. The next you painted me. You looked straight into me, as if you were reaching to know who I am.

My first drawing was in charcoal, smudging in and rubbing out the lines until I found the right expression in your eyes. Staring, I noticed how you grew full of anger when any teacher came near. I understood this look … this break from trust.

I liked the feel of the blackened charcoal stick because it comes from wood and fire… It felt fitting material for us to use. How to describe what I painted? Someone looking brave and strong but at the point of breaking.

When we finished the teacher said we could add one

other thing to the portrait.
Without hesitation I drew
your sister's tree. After,
you painted your hand and
stamped it over the face I
painted. It was a disturbing
image and the teacher was
angry, saying you had no right
to mark my work, telling
you this is exactly the kind of
impulsive behaviour that gets you
into trouble.

But I defended your action. "We are painting portraits
together and this hand over the face makes the portrait
true."

Afterwards you clenched me and whispered,
"Thanks, Om, man. You are the only one who gets me."
Then you laughed a sad laugh with no joy, an echo of
your father's discord in Greenlands tower.

I carried on drawing to complete the picture.
Above you I charcoaled in the two black birds that stayed
by you. "My ravens!" You stretched out your arms like
wings. I thought of your dancing.

All term we continued making portraits of each
other. As we worked together I saw how tired you

were, how lack of sleep came creeping on you, turning your days slowly, slowly into night.

You started using charcoal too but first you painted your page in yellow like a desert in full glare of the sun. I do not like this colour: it is a blast of searchlight in my eyes. My mouth grew dry at the sight of it, my throat scorched with the desert sun reflected from the sand. The endless yellow we walked and walked and walked across in search of green.

In art we found the way to see ourselves and each other beyond the border of language. People do not see enough the truth in the language of eyes.

It felt good to be seen. I sat still as stone when you drew me. I was used to sitting still. Hiding in woodland, crying inside hard enough for feeling in me to reach the stars.

I saw the way the teachers looked on our friendship, suspiciously. Perhaps they thought you were bullying me, or maybe that we were two troubled boys who should not be encouraged to be together.

The young teacher tapped me on the shoulder when I sat for you and said, "Om, don't forget to breathe!" I thought this is something no one needs to tell me.

I realize I have forgotten to breathe as Om tells our story.
"I remember... You asked me why I painted in yellow."

"And you told me it's because that was where our friendship
began when I found you ... broken against the yellow wall
of the Bothy. You will never know how it felt for me, Kai, to
have found a true friend."

Only in art were you settled. There was something
strange in how you gave up just when you should
be working hard for examinations. I moved forward.
I wanted to take you with me into progress, but it seemed
that all I could do was to show you how to paint your way
out of sadness. We did that in the Bothy – you allowing me
to cover the yellow wall. Even there, in our secret place of
art, only in small moments could you find peace.

When Aunt Gisou stood on the balcony with the letter
from the Red Cross, the one we wait for every year for the
four years we have lived here, I tell her to open it because
I cannot. Hope can burn as brutal as hate. It burned so
bright in me that day, but the first word I saw when she
opened it was 'regret'. I collapsed to the floor but Aunt
Gisou said, "No, my nephew. Regret that there is no news,

that is all. Nothing has changed."

But something did change in me that day, because I knew I could not keep looking back. I had been burned too many times by hope. So all my hope I put into you... You were the brother I could help.

In Year Eleven I took trials to join the football team again and finally I got in. I thought maybe Zak had told his father who is coach that he should let me join because my football skills were rusted. Then I understood Zak also wanted to speak through me to you, Kai, to make me a peace flag.

After football Zak asked me please to tell Kai we need him too on the team. "We miss him. I miss him." It is hard sometimes for boys to speak, isn't it? Even when they share the same language, it is hard.

It is different if that language is in your feet and eyes, in the twist of a shoulder or a raised arm on the pitch. I also wished my brother Kai would join us on this precious free land they call a Rec – but no matter what I said you would not. You preferred to dance, but I did not like the way you turned to the beat of your heavy music. Some days your body began to jerk in a strange rhythm, more raven than human. I grew afraid for you.

What I came to learn was that Orla, Zak and Kai were close friends in the past but not now. I did not exactly understand why their bond grew weak. This too I have seen on the road. Pain can bring you close or it can break you. Now it was you and me walking together, painting together, and, because my language was flowing more, speaking together. I couldn't understand why you would no longer play football. I did not understand why you refused to see your old friends again in the Bothy, in these woods you discovered together. My world was growing and this is all I wished for – what you had… To still know the people who I grew up with.

My questions and encouragement to see old friends made you angry and I think suspicious of me. You thought people were talking about you and your family, especially your father. I am sorry, Kai, but my Aunt Gisou spoke of him as the Shadow Man of Greenlands tower. I told her she should not say sharp-tongued things because we too have our ghosts. I did not tell you of these conversations because sometimes Aunt Gisou's path has made her speak hard words, harsh words that do not reveal her softness, the kindness she holds inside. But at that time she became anxious and it was harder for me to see you.

At school you grew in paranoia. Telling me everyone has their eyes on your family, not to get involved, that they would interfere. You would not listen when I told you that they care for you.

I saw it in Zak's eyes he wanted friendship. I told you to forget that this division ever happened but you insisted that the fight with Zak was not the kind of fight so easily forgotten. "Just remember, Om, Zak's from one side of the Rec and we're from the other," you told me. And it sounded foolish, because I have walked over the world, not a small football pitch, but still I saw that the struggle was more than I understood.

"You must have thought I was such an idiot. I never imagined it would be so hard to see myself through your eyes."

I tried hard to understand but I did not know why you were telling me something obvious. That is why I continued to question. "Why does this matter? Why can't Zak and Orla come here? You told me how Bothy means shelter for anyone."

You bitter-laughed at me and said, "You have a lot to learn about this country, Om!" and I felt my own fire inside thinking you don't even know my name Omid, meaning hope. This hope I carried with me like a flame. I questioned how you would survive if you had seen what I have seen.

I knew your ears were closed to me, that I should not

push further but if I was to help you I needed to try so I asked, "Is it because of Orla? Because of jealousy with Zak? I think you love her?"

I stepped back from you, ready to leave the Bothy because by the look in your eyes you would fight me too, but I did not read you well that day. You did not fight and that made me more afraid for you. When I left you shook your head and only said, "Om, you don't understand. It's about everything."

Especially at revision time Aunt Gisou was not happy with my bond with you, Kai. Every day she sensed more fire in it, in you and your family. Every time she saw you not in school she told of her fear that you will bring danger to her door.

After all the experiences I have had she still was not happy for me to go into this small woodland without her. She tried to forbid me to go to the Bothy. Each day her fear grew until she did not even wish me to play football on the Rec. This is something of which we argued. I said, "I am not a child any more." I asked her, "Why did we come here to this country only for you to take my freedom from me?"

I was sorry I raised my voice and to make peace I made her cinnamon tea. Then she told me, "It's OK, Omid. I am proud of you. You must grow in this country. I am finding it more difficult. This season of winter is not good for my mind-health. That is why I am full of fear." I was pulled in two directions because I knew I had to care for her, but I also wished I could go to help you, Kai. And also, yes, I wanted to play football and meet my new friends Zak and Orla. My world was growing.

Something I saw many nights made me think perhaps Aunt Gisou was right to lose trust in you. Small groups of older boys wheeling their bikes down the path to this Bothy and I did not like their look. Boys with shaded faces. Ghost-grey skin, like ash. Boys living in the shadows whose clothes smell strong of drug-weed.

Then came the day when I smelled it on you too and saw it in the hopeless heavy lids of your eyes, like shutters closing.

At school your wild ways and fury mouth were always getting you detainment. It made me afraid for you, my brother.

It felt like an emergency. I thought to myself if one brother is lost I cannot let another slip away. This is why I made a plan to ask Orla and Zak if they will meet me in the Bothy so they could see for themselves. I felt like I was betraying you, my brother, but I knew I must. This was my aim to bring you all back to your old times, to bring us together, because I knew now, with the arrival of these shadow boys, that they wanted something of you … and I could not help you alone. To remind you of who you are I needed the help of your childhood friends.

After my plan was set I did not have to wait many days for you to be in trouble and kept after school for swearing in the face of the temporary art teacher. I told you this is not respectful but I do not think since the shadow boys arrived, bringing their smoke, that you could hear me. Maybe you didn't care.

It was my last idea of how to help you so when the siren went for the end of the day I made sure I was the first through Ravenscroft School gates and out on the Rec. There I waited for Zak and Orla. I saw they were holding hands and looking close into the other's eyes. They were surprised when I called them to ask if they will come with me to the Bothy.

"Did Kai ask for us?" Zak's voice rose, hoping that the idea for this was yours.

I shook my head and pointed into school. Your ravens sat on the school gates, waiting for you to come out. "He is detained again, but you must come with me to see," I explained.

They broke hands and asked no more questions as we walked to Greenlands wood. Like each was thinking their own thoughts, perhaps memories of a past I did not live.

Zak tried first to enter through thick growth. He said the path to the Bothy used to be a "secret short cut when we were kids", but the bush-spikes were too sharp and so we walked along the concrete path to the road, past our flats and down the hill.

Zak tried to hold Orla's hand as we took the path to the Bothy but she pushed him away and sniffed the air. "This place stinks of skunk." She looked to me for the first time, suspiciously. "Do you two smoke in here?"

I shook my head. "Not me. This is why I asked you here. There are others who have started to come... Older boys. I do not know them. They come here on bikes. I see them passing, throwing night-shadows over Greenlands."

The ravens must have got tired of waiting for you at school because they followed us here, making friendly greetings to old friends. I observed the look in Zak's and Orla's eyes, as if they were travelling back in time into a sacred place that was now a ruin. "It used to be so sunny here," Orla whispered.

"It is winter," I said but I saw she did not mean the season.

Quickly I shut the door so the ravens didn't follow as they always want to do. Today the floor was littered with rolled cigarettes and there were sofa stains. I saw also evidence that the ravens now do come inside.

In the gloom-light Kai and Orla stared at the walls. "Is this your art?" Orla wanted to know.

"It is both our art," I told her. "I painted my city and Kai, he painted ravens."

"I don't see a city?" Zak said, picking off a piece of yellow paint.

"Give me that!" Orla said and Zak shrugged and handed it over. There was stress between them.

I saw admiration and shock together in their eyes, and now I realized they were right. It was worse than I thought. My Aleppo sky in miniature that took me one whole year to paint, to remember, was destroyed in red-blood spray. I have to tell you I felt sharp pain in my heart that day, Kai.

I hurt inside, thinking, *How can Kai allow this?* I do not believe my brother would do this to me. "I have never seen this red paint before," I told them "This is new. I think it is the work of shadow boys."

I see deep sorrow in their eyes. But they had no true understanding of me. I hated the yellow brightness that was there before, but it was not my idea to paint it out. I wanted to tell them so because the look Orla gave me that day made me think she blamed me – for the painting out of yellow and the change in you. As if I was a bad influence. She placed her hand on the wall, like she was searching for an old heartbeat.

"I had no idea," Zak said. "We should never have let him push us away."

I tried to explain. "We painted many hours together here. This was survival art but now he needs something different... Some connection with others." In truth I needed it too.

I touched the red spray paint as if it would burn me. "These new visitors are not healthy."

Orla leaned against the wall and told us of a boy she met in a play-den up the hill when she moved into Greenlands. A boy so full of life and happiness that he was like the sun. Zak told of making friendship bonds on the first day of school, of bathing and blowing wish bubbles from your balcony. These stories of sweetness brought tears in all three of us.

I cried also for the memories of my childhood city, my lost friends who will always be strangers to them ... for my lost brother. I told them that the Kai I know would never paint my city out. This is how I knew how lost you were then – that you had allowed it. I saw they felt for me though they did not know all my grief. I told them I have survived worse, but I insisted for them to see what I saw then – the dying light of the hopeless. I have seen it take people too many times to ignore.

"You did the right thing to ask us here," Orla whispers.

"He must not know that I told you. You must not betray him to others. I don't want to make him more trouble. I brought you here to ask of you to find a way to build back your friendship. So we have strength together to offer him." I wished then that I had a chance to show how I climbed trees in our orchards of home when I was a small child. "Even if you aren't children any more, you remember each other as who you were. That is something precious."

We were inside the Bothy only a short time. The ravens sat outside like bodyguards. I thought they were waiting for you, Kai. I told Orla and Zak that it was better that you did not find them here but I am happy they came, because now… I saw it in their eyes, the desperation and determination that everything must change.

When I walked up the hill past the Sula tree a silver leaf touched my skin and my thought was clear. I knew I had done a good thing – some secrets are too poisonous to keep.

Days turned. Winter grew colder. Zak found me and Orla one break time. He told us that Kai is in more trouble because he did not attend detention. From my count this was the fifth time he was shunned from school – one time excluded for his fighting, three times suspended, also many times detained. Zak tried to find out how much trouble. "Mum said the head teacher is being patient with him because of the family situation but if he carries on this way he'll be expelled. Have you seen this?"

Zak showed us an article cut from the news. I read it over Orla's shoulder and I realized I understood almost every word now. It said the council planned to turn the Rec into a new estate because of a shortage in housing.

Zak shook his head. "They can't do this. The school's going to challenge it. What about the football pitch? We hardly have any space at school as it is."

But I saw the look in Orla's eye, that she and I did not think of football. In my mind I saw only Greenlands wood and you, Kai. I understood straight away from the computer-made map at the bottom of the article showing the boundary on the new plan for buildings. The road cut through our wood.

I pointed to the grey block that is our flat and the 'access road' that would cross the wood, through the place where Sula's tree is planted, through the Bothy into a new place called the Greenhaven Estate with three new blocks of housing.

Once more I saw understanding in Orla's eyes. Her mouth was tight, green eyes sharp with anger. We were thinking the same. *This will break Kai.*

I also thought how Aunt Gisou loved this wild space. I thought of my Aleppo sky painted out and I had this strong feeling. I told them, "This is an opportunity out of difficulty. We must take this news to Kai, to my aunt, to your families, and we must fight for all our sakes."

After school I headed straight to the Bothy. It stank and music was coming from inside but I heard no shadow voices so I went in. You tried to stand against the wall to mask the graffiti.

I handed you the article. Your eyes were drug clouded. It seemed as if nothing of this news could touch you until I made you understand that you would lose Sula's tree. Only then you woke up. "Over my dead body. This wilderness is mine and Dad's. We discovered it. They can't take this away from us."

I told you that Orla and Zak wanted to meet you to work out how to save this land.

"Not here!" Your eyes were panic-full. I saw in a flash you were seeing yourself as they would … and I knew you cared. Still had pride. *This is good,* I thought.

"Tell them to meet me after school tomorrow at Sula's tree," you said, and I was happy you had not slipped too far away to pull back.

Then you stepped away from the defiled wall and shook your head. "I'm sorry, Om. This wasn't me. I should have thrown them out."

I took your hand. "This is no way to repay the kindness I have given you. I can paint again but still it will not take me home. My land is lost to me but you must fight this, for your sister, for your family too, for me, Aunt Gisou and Orla. For this is the ground where your sister is planted. Now where we too are planted. This is our Greenlands."

Then speaking low, as if digging somewhere for the Kai of distant memory, you said, "We have to be Greenlands Guardians, cutting through the dark. Like when we were kids." I did not understand exactly your meaning but that night I slept peacefully through the night.

I woke to the cold, bright blue-sky morning of hope and it made the flame in me burn stronger. Walking past your door, I wished you would not be suspended any more. I willed all day for you to keep your appointment on our Green Hill.

I met Zak and Orla outside the school gates. My heart was full of happiness to see you waiting for us, sitting by the Sula tree. I was relieved you did not smell of bitter herbs that day. Your eyes were shining clear but I saw that you were nervous, transferring weight from foot to foot.

I observed this meeting closely, like a moment in history, a truce between friends. I was happy feeling that I was the peacemaker who brought you back to childhood bonds.

"I heard you've got a sister," you said, and Zak looked at his feet. "What's her name?"

"Hope." It came out as a choked whisper and you kept tight hold of Zak's hand.

"Kai, man, your hands are ice blocks!" Zak said, pulling away. "How long have you been waiting here?"

"Too long," you said. "Me and the ravens have been having a little conference! Working out what we're going to do."

Zak and Orla laughed a little. I was not tuned for jokes but I felt the power of this reunion and I felt sure in this moment that if we stand all together then those other shadows could not so easily descend.

Many things were said, all of it I understood, maybe better than any of you. I listened. I observed and recorded pictures of a time before I arrived in my mind.

These are the words I will always remember Orla said:

"This land is our past, our future."

Only one thing I had to add…

I interrupt Om – his words seared on my mind. "I remember what you said… It is our present."

We held each other in the embrace of brothers. And I thought that here at the roots of this purifying tree is where all our stories can meet together. Zak walked away to the other side of the Rec and I followed you and Orla back to our Greenlands. For the first time since I arrived in this country I felt like I belonged.

I stood on the balcony that night, searching the moon, thinking of my old life. The ravens flew to your balcony and one of them stared at me with its shining eye. I saw this clearly about us– we were like a delicate friendship tower, trust between us was just starting to build.

With one balcony stacked on another.
Me at the top,
Orla in the middle
and you, Kai, beneath, were the foundation.

And I felt a rush of happiness that we were strong together.
Because I know this to be true:
if foundations fall
all
will
fall.

Kai

As I finish recording Om's passage of writing he passes me a thick envelope with my name on it. "Orla instructed me to give you this, only when I had completed my part. She said for you to listen to the inbetween notes of all our tellings and then you will reach the truth. She told me you will understand her meaning."

I do.

She's written my name on the envelope and just seeing it written in her handwriting sends me spinning.

Orla

No *indrucing* needed! You asked for this!

Since we were kids Greenlands has always been our turf, hasn't it? Yours, mine, Zak's, your mum and dad's... Om's too now. Whatever thorny paths we've had to clear we've done it together. It's our garden, planted with childhood wishes, trial kisses! Our Greenlands paradise. What did you call it once? "Our very own little low heaven." It's true that's what it was for us when we were kids – swing-spinning, den-building, discovering the Bothy. This is where we hatched all our sunshine dreams even when it rained. And then came the growing pains and the working out of what we were to each other... Like that kiss I sprang on you because we were just so happy the day Sula was born even though you've really always been more my brother. Then the heartache of Sula's death was such a sudden change. Not just for you either, Kai. It felt like till that time we'd just been playing at life. Maybe it's not only you who needs to write this out.

Anyway, then came planting Sula's tree and the raw ache of your dad trying to play his music but never producing more than that tormented wail. I'll never forget the look on your face that memorial day, covering your ears as if that could shield you from the pain. I felt pulled in every direction because Zak wanted to come so badly to see you, to plant the tree together, but you were already pushing him away. You know what he told me once? He felt guilty, but sometimes, if it meant he was going to lose you he wished his mum weren't pregnant. He said he cared more about you than a baby brother or sister he hadn't met yet.

This is hard to say, Kai, but if you really need to see it from my point of view this isn't going to be an easy read. There was never going to be a short cut to walking back into the sunshine. Your ravens (and by then I thought of them as yours) were landing on Greenlands railings like they never had before.

And with them and Sula dying came Om. When Faith gave me that mentor role of helping Om settle in it was so awkward. I saw his strange silences and I think in my head I sort of connected you and your family losing everything with Om arriving. It felt to me as though his silence had settled on us all from above and was seeping down through our block. I shouldn't have been, but I was kind of angry and maybe even a bit jealous when you and he got close because I couldn't work out how or why you would cut us out and let in an almost silent stranger.

Mum said she was sure you broke down because your family couldn't cope with Zak's mum having baby Hope so soon after Sula dying. She said that Janice couldn't look her in the eye these days. Even if they bumped into each other at work, she avoided her. Then there was your dad… We only heard him, hardly ever going out. Playing those single wrenching notes, bleeding all our hearts and keeping us awake at night. If it wasn't him it was you drowning us out with your beats blasting out of the Bothy. We all understood, or thought we did, but you didn't make it easy for anyone.

What really did it was the way you had of looking at us like we were all suddenly your enemies.

We tried to help you, me and Zak. Who do you think persuaded his mum to get so involved? Who do you think kept pleading for them to give you another chance, or suggested you see the therapist woman? Zak was always there for you, always had your back whenever you got into trouble, again and again and again. No matter how hard we tried, the only person you'd spend any time with was Om. Zak even tried to take some detentions for you, when his mum was on maternity leave, so you wouldn't get into more trouble. Bet he still hasn't told you! One day maybe you'll ask him for his story. You should do.

"Give Kai time," my mum would say, but time drifted by and you only got worse. Days, then months, then years of time at secondary flew by and apart from nodding if our paths crossed, and cringing in pain every time I went out and didn't call for you, we drifted, didn't we ... you, me and Zak?

None of us really saw what was going on inside your flat. I mean, we knew your dad wasn't working or even playing his music then and your mum was thin and wired with all the extra shifts she took on.

But my mum felt it wasn't right to intrude so we sensed rather than saw this pressure building inside Greenlands. Now we know what you were living with I think we should have intruded. It must have been hell for you watching your dad "slowly slipping into his shadow skin", as you call what happened to him. We should have seen it coming. It's obvious now he was crying out for help, howling through the building.

It was like bit by bit your family sealed itself off. We weren't welcome any more. Without ever saying it our Bothy was off limits for us, and yes, I did resent that. Whenever I stood on our balcony, looking down over Greenlands, all I could think of was working out a way to get through to you, especially with all the trouble you started getting in. The Kai you were then didn't feel like the you I'd known since we were kids.

We were all breaking apart when we should have been pulling together, and I felt like I was in the middle of this tug of war between you and Zak... Zak and me were always more because it was safe and I could trust him. I just wanted to live on the sunny side. The day that Hope was born... It was about being near happiness and me being with Zak was really always about that. I wasn't choosing him over you. I was choosing happiness.

Anyway, it was frightening to see your rage and Zak got the full force of it. The way you looked then, Kai, the anger in your eyes... Even Mum said I should steer clear of you. She got quite worked up about it, said she wouldn't have me spoiling my chances at school by putting all my energies into you. We argued a lot. I told her she was a hater, selfish, heartless... She said she'd seen this story too many times before and she wasn't going to let her daughter get caught up in it.

In the end we were all wrong about lots of things, but especially about Om. When he reached out to me and Zak and showed us what was going on in the Bothy we saw that you'd been trying to help each other and he cared about you as much as we did, maybe more.

I have never felt so guilty as I did that day when Om took us to the Bothy to show us the true state of you. I laid my hands against the wall where once we painted our sunshine hands and I knew then we had to find a way to remember what we were to each other and to this place. We couldn't scrape the time away and go back there but we had to get you to fight for yourself.

Strange how all our friendship bonds together are somehow connected to the Bothy and our little bit of Greenlands wildness. I was thinking the other day … it's like this bit of land keeps trying to bring us together and help us grow. Like it's always had our backs. Weird how, when the news came of the plans for a road to run through it, it gave us a problem but for a moment it gave us an answer too, of sparking the life in you again, bringing you back to us. But it was such a fleeting moment.

You have no idea how happy it made me to meet you at Sula's tree. You, me, Zak and Om and for the first time in years I saw the old you, Kai. You didn't know we'd seen the state of the Bothy but it didn't matter. I saw you still cared. What was that little rhyme you used to chant about the ravens? Well, it was the first time in years I had seen the shine in your eyes, Kai, and it gave me hope.

That night, before I went to sleep, I thought how true

it is what people say… It's only really when something's being taken from you that you realize how precious it is.

Kai

I can't read on, not because I don't want to but because my eyes are so blurred with tears. It was hard enough to write my own parts but I had no idea how much it would cut me up seeing my fall through Om's and Orla's eyes… Great sobs gush out of me at the memory of hope and possibility in that moment of reunion Orla described and thinking what could have been if… If I could pick up the pen and write a different ending. If I could change my story. But then that would be running away again and I would not be who I am now, writing this.

I unfurl myself from the curled-up foetus huddle I find myself in and slip Orla's writing back inside the envelope, because I don't think I can take any more just now, but something's blocking it from lying flat. I peer inside and find a tiny plaster-fragment of secret sunshine … to hold while I write on.

Next time they come,
Taz and Zig,
with their offerings of forgetting,
smoke rings of oblivion,
I'll show them the door.
We don't need this any more.
Dad doesn't need this.
If I can get him to remember
how we were Greenlands Guardians,
how we cleared this wood.
Me and Dad.
How we hacked our way through the brambles until the sun
flooded in
then maybe he'll see that we could do it again.
I close my eyes,
wrap my arms round myself.
Sometimes it's like I can feel Sula's warmth,
smell her sweet, soapy skin.
Holding Sula
in my heart,
I rock us together.

Through the broken slat in the door of the Bothy,
through the archway of our old den,
I spy her tree.

At the threshold the raven pair peek in,
heads tilted, questioning.
This day everything changes.
After tonight
no more smoke.
After tonight.
Tell Taz and Zig
not to come here
any more.
Clear the Bothy out,
make an effort at school,
paint the walls clean again.
Start over altogether.
After tonight.
After—

Taz's wheels skid into the door.
The chipped wood cracks.
I'm ready for them.
"Fancy a smoke? What do you let those ravens in for?"
Taz waves his puny arms over his head. "They stink!"
"You stink!"
He shrugs and starts to roll.
We don't talk much ever really,
not to each other.

Sometimes we have a rant in our own little worlds.
This is not about talking.
He hands me a smoke.
"Giving it up," I say.
He turns and looks at me with glazed eyes. "Come off it,
Kai, man!"
"Serious!" I say, staring at the state of the walls.
How could I let them do this to Om?
It's freezing in here and we're both shivering.
When he gets I mean it
he doesn't hang around for long.
"Suit yourself! See you around!"
That was easier than I thought.
I suppose he's too stoned to put up a fight.

I camp out in the Bothy,
falling asleep and waking early
to a blast of morning birdsong
and my heart swells with this new fight in me.
Little low heaven.
Little low heaven.
Through our archway den,
little low heaven.
Walking up the hill to Sula's tree,
no one can take this from me.

Sula's silver leaves catch the morning light
and wave.
My head is clear for the first time in ages.
"Time to be Greenlands Guardians again!" I tell the ravens
as they follow me home.
And then I hear the wrenching note of pain.
The raven pair careers past me,
flying skyward,
screeching out their warnings
at the silver glare of Dad's sax falling.

Omid

The hopeful feeling after our meeting lasted only one night. I am sickened to remember it.

I woke, opened my balcony door to see bright morning. Orla was returning from her run but suddenly she slowed. Her face was like ash. Mouth fell wide open. Fear sparked from her. She raised her arm. I leaned over the balcony, turning with my back against the railings. I thought I was dreaming that a raven had grown giant and was taking flight over Greenlands, but then I saw those wings were hands. No raven reflection on the roof over our heads, but a man on the point of falling.

Orla approached Greenlands, both arms stretched up. She called your name. Urgent. Kai, Kai, Kai, Kai. Her cries and the screeches of raven birds joined as one.

You came running from the wood and now you were on the path below. I was surprised to see you out so early. I felt relief it was not you above our flat on the roof. I saw it all through the horror in your eyes. I wanted to come to you, my friend, but I could not move. My hands gripped to the balcony railings.

Heavy running feet above us on the roof. I heard another man speaking and your father, his deep voice... The other man was speaking softly, softly.

Below I saw you pick up the fallen instrument to protect it, all the time your eyes were raised to the roof in fear.

That is all I saw and heard because I closed my eyes, as fire burned inside.

No, no, no, no.

This is the problem when it comes, this trauma stress. Even if you say it is in the past, it flames in the present again.

Shelling is in my head.
My ears.
No, no. Please no.
No more
to hear the thud,
the sound of fear,
of falling.

Aunt Gisou knew. "Come, breathe, Omid. Breathe together." She held me so tight and would not let me go until the shaking ended.

It was quiet above our heads. Aunt Gisou took my hands and pulled them from my face. "It is over," she told me. "No one is hurt."

I uncovered my ears to hear a siren. We walked to the window and saw below that there were police, an ambulance too. I breathed again, feeling relief not to see the shattered ends of life, to see your father was alive but broken, climbing inside an ambulance.

You were screeching like a wounded bird. I wanted to be at your side, my brother, to help you, but Aunt Gisou would not allow it. "Omid, we have carried too much burden already. These are not our people."

She was wrong.

Orla

I will never, ever forget that run. It was one of those bright blue-sky winter mornings. When everything felt fresh and clean. Greenlands was laced with ice and Sula's tree dazzled in the early morning sunshine. *The things that have happened have happened*, I thought, and we can't go back. But there can still be sunshine...

Then I turned the corner to Greenlands and heard the ravens crackling, grawking, screeching, their wild-wings beating as your dad stood on the roof ledge, arms outstretched like he thought he was on the point of flying too.

And then you came running. Picking up your dad's sax and clinging on to it. I don't even know if you felt me by your side, holding our breath as if we shared the same lungs. Every second like a year till finally Frankie from the block over managed to coax your dad down before the ambulance came. You talk of foreshadowings... As you clung to me I had this awful feeling that something had died in you. And after that trauma Greenlands fell silent again. Even the ravens gave up their racket.

The next day your mum, who hadn't been round to ours since Sula died, came banging on our door, pretty aggressively actually. Mum had already gone to work so I was on my own but I could hear how upset she was. To be honest I was a bit afraid to open the door.

When I let her in she wouldn't even have a cup of tea or sit down. I asked after your dad but she didn't want to talk. Just told me in a strange flat voice that he'd been sectioned for his own safety, was in a psychiatric hospital and she wasn't sure how long he'd need to stay there.

I told Janice that Mum was planning to call round and see her later but she shook her head and said, "Tell her not to bother. It's you I'm here to see. I'd thank you not to spread gossip about our family."

I had no idea what she meant. Her eyes were bloodshot with tiredness and tears and hurt and I didn't want to upset her any more so I kept quiet.

"I won't be sitting at your table again! Tell Holly that!" Her voice was bitter as she handed me a letter with the school's crest on it. "The hospital found this in Dexter's pocket. Looks like it sent him over the edge... Here, you read it! He used to call you his three musketeers. Call yourself Kai's friend. Ever heard of sticking together?

Post it through my letterbox when you're done … if it doesn't burn your fingers. I don't want anything more to do with anyone round here and I shouldn't think Kai will either." Then she slammed the door and she was gone.

My hands were shaking as I picked up the envelope.

Dear Mr and Mrs King,

With reference to our ongoing communications and following our most recent meeting concerning your son Kai King, having been informed of his unsociable behaviour outside school, it is the decision of the board that for the welfare of Kai, his fellow students and teaching staff the best course of action is for him to continue his GCSE studies at home with the assistance and guidance of off-site school counsellors who will be made available to him. A social worker will also be contacting you in the coming days. Please contact us for advice on how Kai can enter exams and the centres at which he can—

I couldn't read on. I ran to my room and didn't come out for the rest of the day. All I could think of was who would tell the school. Not Om or his aunt surely. Unless … Zak spoke to his mum about what we saw in the Bothy?

It was my time to be full of rage – I couldn't believe

Zak would be such a snake. Not since Sula died had I felt such pain inside and fear too, because just days ago the world seemed like it could be new again, that we all stood together, and now... Because of this betrayal we'd be split apart forever.

I ran past your door later that day, praying I wouldn't see you. I sprinted to Zak's across the Rec, tears streaming down my face. His mum answered the door. "Orla, what's the matter?"

I was so out of breath I could hardly speak. "Where's Zak?" I threw the letter at her. "If you really want to know what's the matter Kai's dad tried to jump off the roof of Greenlands this morning."

Faith's hands trembled as she led me in.

Zak came running down the stairs, a grin on his face, surprised to see me, and then, at the state of me, he froze.

"What the hell were you doing telling your mum about the Bothy? She went straight to the school."

With all the raised voices Hope began to cry. "Why is Orlie shouting? Orlie cuddle, Orlie cuddle." She stood at the top of the steps, arms outstretched towards me.

Zak's dad appeared next to her and scooped her into his arms, taking in the situation.

"Please, Orla, you're in shock, have a seat. I want you to hear this." Faith sat down at the kitchen table. "Zak raised a concern with me in confidence because he was worried for Kai's welfare." Faith reached out to take my hand but I pulled away. "Orla, I had to inform the school that the family was going through the mill, especially after all the incidents with Kai, and they decided that it might be better for him to get help outside of school services."

She kept shaking her head and saying, "That poor family," and it made me want to leave. I couldn't even look at Zak as he tried to explain why he'd done what he'd done.

Just as I was leaving, little Hope came bumping on her bottom down the stairs, raising her hands in the air for me to pick her up. "I can't. I have to go." I tried to smile at Hope but failed.

Faith followed me to the door. "Zak begged me not to tell anyone but I was duty-bound to inform the school... I see how awful it must have been to get that letter."

"What you see now doesn't make any difference! It's too late. We don't need your pity," I shouted and stormed out.

Zak tore after me but I wouldn't let him walk me home over the Rec. I must have heard your voice in my head because I shrieked at him to stick to his own. I'm not proud of it but I was glad to see the look of hurt in his eyes, though none of it was his fault.

Then you know how we tried, all of us in our own ways,

to spend time with you, call on you. I calmed down after I'd spoken to Zak, and I understood why he did what he did after he'd seen the Bothy. He did it because he was frightened for you.

"Get lost!" you used to shout at us whenever we came knocking. You didn't want anything to do with the Greenlands Guardians meetings Faith was organizing. I felt sorry for her because she really cared about you, Kai. I think she got so involved in the campaign to show you how sorry she was for having any part in you being forced out of school.

And really nothing would have taken off without Zak's parents. Getting the councillor to come along wouldn't have happened without Faith and Joel. Even Om's aunt wanted to help with the campaign, dropping over a list of trees planted there that she says are precious and rare.

The first Greenlands Guardians meeting went badly because the councillor said there had already been a survey of the trees and the access route would not require any of the older trees to be uprooted. I wanted to tell her about Sula's tree, about our den and what the Bothy meant to us, but I knew that none of that emotional stuff would count. Faith said we must be patient and continue to build our arguments against the new development. Being in those meetings, seeing how that stuff works, is what made me want to do law at uni. Strange really how Faith was trying to bring you back into the fold and got me motivated instead.

We had loads of work from school and so that was how Zak and me met now, in meetings about saving the Rec.

Kai

I pick up a leaflet on the mat.

Greenlands Guardians
'Save the Rec' campaign

It feels like a year ago instead of days that we were standing there together, making plans to run this campaign. Me, Om, Zak and Orla. I laugh at myself, never learning not to hope, thinking I could maybe start again ... put things right. Then I get an idea. I pass Mum the flyer. "Maybe I'll show Dad this?"

She shrugs. "Don't get your hopes up, Kai. Your dad's not well." She shakes her head. "He's deeply unwell."

Two weeks feels like a year without him. It's the longest we've ever been apart.

Sectioned.
My dad,
sectioned.
Wings clipped.
Unbalanced.
Taken away for his own safety.

We sit outside the room and wait to visit him. The doctor comes out and closes the door. He sits beside my mum and me like we're his patients too. "Kai?" he half asks, half checks our names against his paperwork.

"I understand this may be difficult for you after waiting for this visit. Dexter thought he was ready but he's become distressed again in the last couple of hours and we've had to calm him. In my opinion he'll need considerably more time. There are triggers…"

Am I a trigger?
Dad's behind that closed door and doesn't want to see me or Mum.
The doctor says sometimes it is best for the patient
to be apart
to reset
restart.
Words echo,
amplified, new and strange.

"Sometimes," he tells us, "it is too painful for patients to
reconnect."
He says this with a sad smile that he keeps on his face like a
shield,
like now he's Dad's bodyguard.
I want to grab hold of the doctor and shake him.
I want to bash my fists into his chest,
barge past him,
fling open the door,
grab my dad
and bring him home.

But the door
that my dad is behind
is closed to me.
Everything is.

Mum goes into a small office to talk to the doctor some more and leaves me sitting out in the cold white-tiled corridor.

This is how I feel – on the outside of everything.

On our way home, staring out of the bus window I wait for Mum to speak. After a while she quietly hands me a letter. "You knew this was coming, didn't you? You've had plenty of warnings. They told me you were running out of options after the last suspension…"

I only have to clock the official Ravenscroft letterhead to know what this is.

"I tried to hide the details of the trouble you've been getting in from your dad but now he knows it all. They found the letter in his pocket. Turns out he's got it all wrong. He thinks *he's* being thrown out. The doctor reckons it's triggered memories of his own school days, such as they were."

Too shocked to speak I read it over. All the 'incidents' I've been 'involved' in listed and numbered. Thirty-three apparently.

I can't breathe.

My mouth is dry as sandpaper.

"You mean he tried to jump because of me? Then I really am the trigger."

Mum wraps her hands round her stomach, like she's imagining Sula's still safe inside. "No, Kai, not you. I wasn't saying… That's just not true. We should talk more, share our troubles."

All I see are the shadows under Mum's eyes.

They're deep,
like bruises.
How can any of us ever sleep peacefully again?
Replaying over and over
the day Sula drifted into a sleep she never woke from.

Mum scrunches her eyes closed and the tears roll slowly down her cheeks. I hear this sound wrench from my chest, like a clod of dry clay breaking up, breaking out of me so I can breathe again.

"Mum! You can talk to *me*," I cry out to her, louder, fiercer than I meant to.

I swap seats and wrap my arm round Mum's shoulder. "It's all such a mess, Kai," she whispers and rests her head against mine.

My chest heaves. I straighten my back and then I see it. Just like Om says he has to look after his Aunt Gisou,

I get it now – I have to look after Mum. I have to make it right. "Don't cry, Mum, please. I'll help you." I pick up the envelope. "I'll sort myself out and get back into school."

Mum doesn't even open her eyes but pats my knee like she used to when I was a kid. "I love you, Kai," she says.

"Love you too, Mum." I say the words that used to come automatically, and the fire inside dampens down enough for my mind to clear like it hasn't since Sula died.

I exhale the pain. "I'm really going to try. By the time Dad gets out of there I'll be back in school doing my GCSEs. I'm going to make you proud."

Mum takes the letter from me. "Who's been talking about us? That's what I want to know. Spies in our own home... Either Orla or Janice, or I suppose it could be that Gisou. I've seen the judgy way she looks at me. But you're right, Kai, we've got each other. We can cope. I'm going to sort the flat out, so when Dad's well again and comes back home we can make a fresh start. I might get someone in to help sort the place..."

"I'll do it, Mum. We don't need anyone around. Just you and me."

"No, Kai. You crack on with your revising and get yourself back into school," she says and there it is again, that doubt in her eye. I get it... Once the idea's planted that I'm a waster I see it in everyone, even in Om.

And now the moment of peace has passed the fire's rising again, flaming through my insides. The seed of doubt is planted in me too.

My mind tracks back to
the football pitch when Dad lost it.
After Sula...
Never playing his sax again.
To the rant about the ravens' wings,
losing it with that Ravenmaster.
Back to his song-weaving,
wasteland clearing,
singing his lungs out.
The way he curled in on himself whenever he had to come
to school.
Glaring at the teachers like they were his enemies,
even the ones I liked,
telling me how he can sniff it out –
racism.
The weird things he'd sometimes say.
I remember
Mum hushing him.
Telling him to stop filling my head with nonsense,
to stop loading his growing pains on me.
Now the earth-wrenching note of his dented sax chimes

through me.
Don't fear the ravens, Kai.
Look to the shine in their eye.

Minor chords play me, casting doubt on all the things I loved in him too.

The wilderness of confusion is clearing... But it's such a long journey home. He's so far away – a bus and a train and a tube. It's dark when we get back and I stand in front of my mirror, searching for the buried shine in my own eye... "What if I've lost it too?"

There it is, the question that has not been spoken.
Bald, open, out there.
Stark as the raven's cry cutting through night.
"Just going out for a walk," I say and again I see the doubt-cast in Mum's eye.

In the Bothy,
imagining again
what I have promised,
not to smoke.
It's floating through my mind.
Can I stop?

I form my mouth into an O
and pop the non-existent smoke rings out.
They float and melt, float and melt.
Nothing is sectioned for its own safety here.
I crank my speaker up instead.
Have to find some way to lose myself.

I turn a slow somersault.
Blood rushes to my head.
This dance is the nearest I get
to swimming back into safe waters with Sula.
The nearest I get to
flying with ravens.
Gliding into the sun
or out of it.
I back bend,
body fold,
pushing off with my feet
in a slow, slow somersault.
Wrists give way,
brain sways.

"Watch out!" Taz shouts as I career into him and Zig.
Where did they come from? "Heard what happened to your
dad – that's a bad scene, mate."

"I'm not your mate!"

"Whatever. We're here for you, me and Zig. Don't see anyone else around unless you're counting ravens now?" Taz sneers. "Here! We brought a stash to get you through. Looks like you could do with it."

"I told you. I don't want it and I can't pay. You've got to stop bringing those bikes down here. I don't want any of it." I hand the smoke back but he won't take it.

Taz drops his butt on the floor. The embers glow. "Now, Kai, have we ever charged you for anything?"

"I told you I don't want it any more. Stop coming here..."

"Your choice!" he mutters, but kicks the door hard so it cracks. I back away. "You told me the Bothy's free for anyone to come and go. Isn't that so, Zig?"

"That's what I thought!" Zig nods like the sidekick puppet he is.

And with that they walk out, leaving the stash on the floor and new bikes leaning against the wall. "Be seeing you around, mate!" Taz calls back.

I watch the embers die,
close my eyes
to blast away the vision of my dad, arms spread like raven
wings,
ready to leap.

Not allowed to see him.
Not allowed to speak to him
for his own safety.
It's for the best.
"Just for now."
"Just till things settle."
What the hell is that supposed to mean?
"For his recovery."
Sectioned.
Even the word sounds like a knife,
like being dissected,
and turns out I'm his trigger.
My chest aches in emptiness.
Just one smoke then...
I stir myself,
unroll the bundle
carefully,
so when I give it back
they'll never know
that it's been touched.
I scrabble around for roach
but give up.
Watch my fingers rolling
crumbs of stale tobacco.
Seal it tight enough.

Light the flint.
Take in a long, slow draw,
sealing the stash.

If Taz comes back
I'll hand it over
and he won't know
I owe him anything.

When I crawl out again,
floating up the hill,
Om's standing by the old den with his aunt.
Walking round Sula's tree.
I'm through the archway now,
too late to hide even if I had the energy.

"Sorry, Kai, for problems with your father," Om says. "We came here thinking to plant a tree, for hope of my brother, Ishy."

"No news then?" I ask him.

"No news. This way or the other." He turns away to speak to his aunt.

She shakes her head and takes Om by the arm, sniffs the air suspiciously and leads him away from me.

But in that moment I know. Om has seen how I am.

Orla

From when your dad went away you were absent too, and I don't just mean from school. I saw the social worker and the counsellors knocking at your door so I thought maybe you were getting help. I even braved it to the Bothy one night but went away when I heard you in there with what Om called your 'shadow mates', their bikes dumped outside the door and rank smoke stinking the air.

We could have been living on opposite sides of the world instead of a floor away from each other. It sounds pathetic now but with Greenlands Guardians meetings at Faith's, exams to do and my mum banging on about keeping to my own course, time just passed and the only thing I could do was block it all out. The worst moment of every day was when I walked past your door. It made me have to toughen up and, as I did, this strange mix of resentment and guilt kicked in. I felt so sad for you but I wanted to shake you too because we were fighting so hard to save our little piece of land and you seemed set on wrecking it. I just got my head down and lost myself in work and trying to save our little plot of green. I expect you didn't even know or care that all this was going on.

We had this formal meeting at the council that they called a First Stage Community Consultation. They said the planning application was a long drawn-out process and that they would take all our points into consideration but that there was also a clamouring need for "affordable housing". One councillor raised the fact that part of the problem was that the land below Greenlands was starting to attract antisocial behaviour. That was you and your new Bothy mates he was talking about, Kai.

I was at home revising more and more and I realized that it wasn't silence filling the Greenlands tower but rage. As far as I could tell Frankie from over the way, who saved your dad's life, was trying to help your mum out. Cleaning things up a bit in the flat, but I heard how you lost it with him.

Kai

Not everything travels on sound waves.

This is how it is when my dad's away "recovering".

I'm counting the days, the weeks, the months till Dad comes home.

Om calls sometimes, Orla too, quietly knocking at the door. But I can't have them seeing me. Not like this.

The fire inside won't let me work. No revision done, no matter how hard I try. In any case, to revise you've got to have learned it the first place, right?

What's the point anyway? But, as far as Mum's concerned, never fear ... Frankie's here!

Fireman Frankie – strong but mild, gentle giant, oh so kind. Local hero, life-saver, friend and helper... Too good to be true.

But what no one sees or hears from any of their balconies (not even Mum) are Frankie's arms of steel or his heart of stone. What people see is my dad's saviour. Everybody witnessed that. And now Frankie is Mum's saviour too. I think he gets off on saving people. He likes that Mum, Dad and me will be forever in his debt.

With Dad away Fireman Frankie seems a bit too keen to step in. Shining a light on everything my dad isn't. The longer Dad's away, the further he gets his feet under the table.

Dad's not having any visitors for now. It's easier that way, for Mum anyway. Sometimes when she puts on her cheery make-up mask in the morning, smearing on a pink smile, I wonder if she even thinks of Dad. Their 'discussions' from way back echo in my ear – "for what he's worth, for what he's worth..." Old word-wounds bleed into me too, morphing... "For what I'm worth, what am I worth?" In this flat, now that Sula's gone and Dad too, I wonder what is the point of me?

Mum gave Frankie keys to our flat so he can drop in while she's at work.

I can see in everyone's eyes that they think he's just what I need. What I've been missing – a strong male safeguarding influence. I get taken off 'cause for concern' on one of the social worker's forms. He always gets ticks in their book – "supported by friends and neighbours..." Phew! Now they can ease off 'post crisis' attention.

Mum's working shifts and Frankie too. Then they switch.
Ah, Frankie.
Thanks, Frankie.
I don't know how I would have managed without you, Frankie.
Makes me want to stick my fingers down my throat and puke, Frankie.
Wheedling his way in,
too good to be true, won't take my eyes off of you.

"He's only offering to support a friend. No need for all the hostility." I can't believe Mum's taking his side over me.

One day he goes too far, steps over the line. Tries to get me to clean my room. "You're not my dad!" I yell at him, smashing my fist into the wall next to his head. "You can't tell me what to do!" It feels so good to see him flinch.

It sparks again and again, the rage, the burning and the fire inside that no one, especially not Frankie, can put out.

I see when Frankie's here the way he plays it. All calm and firm and fatherly. Mum's butter in his hands. But when she's out it starts again, the rage in me, and I've discovered there's rage in Frankie too. It's satisfying to goad it out of him.

"No! I'm not your dad. I only saved his life!" Frankie hurls at me, hurt that I won't put him on a pedestal. He jabs on, words flying like punches. "I'd watch out if I were you. I'd say the apple didn't fall far from the tree…"

I am quiet then, wishing again to crawl under the earth with Sula.

Afterwards he says sorry, "for speaking out of turn". But what he thinks of me is out there now. The scab's been picked.

When Mum gets home I decide to come out with it. "I don't want Frankie having our keys, and I don't think Dad would either."

She looks at me as if I'm far away, as if I understand nothing. Now I wish I could goad her too, break through her mask. "Your dad doesn't know what he wants. Frankie's a real rock to me right now."

"I bet he is!" I snap and her hand flashes across the space between us.

Tears sting her eyes, like she's the one who's just been slapped. But it's too late. I've seen the flash of hatred in her eyes where once there was only love.

Mum has never in her life hit me before and now the pained tears pool in both our eyes.

She reaches out straight away but I lash back at her. "I should have died instead of Sula! You'd be happy then!"

And I see the dull, flat look on her face. I see that we are a family of broken blue sky, fragments of crushed hope, our sunshine painted out.

She says nothing. Her smile has faded away with the exhaustion of her day and she doesn't even try to argue with me. Just takes herself off to bed. I know now I was right, because Sula was all love and light and Mum hates the sight of me. Not that I blame her, because mostly I hate the sight of myself.

Mum's light stays on. She's probably taken her pill and fallen asleep with the lamp on. Without the light and the pill she doesn't sleep. "You have your drugs, I have mine!" I told her that once, but it wasn't appreciated.

In-som-ni-a.
The name of a land you can't trust,
fire, fire, under your feet
every step of the way.
Smoke silent-wreathing into lungs.
If Sula can fall asleep wrapped snug in her cot and never
wake up then we can too.

Maybe I could close my eyes and never wake.
Slip away quietly in my sleep.
Maybe that would be best for everyone.

Today, like every day, Mum's movements are crisp as her nurse's uniform, her armour. I watch her from the balcony. I see it now. She's the warrior fighting to survive, visiting Sula's tree like she does every day. Visiting the dead and forgetting the living.

I open the door to the Bothy.
No more Orla,
no more Zak

blowing bath bubbles
over the Rec.
Not even Om's art to disappear into any more.
Come back to us, Dad, come back, I wish on the rainbow orb
of memory bubbles.

It bursts
like it always did, like it always does.

Omid

Kai. I did not abandon you. I could not go to the Bothy.
I did not have the strength. I also understand that
sometimes there are no words. No matter what help is
offered and how many people try. I saw Zak visit you there
one day. But somehow I knew not one of these people could
break through your armour. I understood. Understand.
There is safety in silence.

Each day I watched you with your shadow mates slip
deeper under your shadow skin. Sometimes on my way to
school I saw you dancing with ravens. I thought maybe you
were sleeping in the Bothy, lost in smoke fog. With each
day's dawn my heart broke to see you. From my balcony I
noticed how you began to move your head, this way and that
way, as if you and they had understanding of each other.

I hope you can understand now I needed to fight my own
fires... If I came too close I feared that I too would burn.

In art I was painting fire. Zak's mum was the main
teacher now she had returned. Sometimes I found her on
the path taking her small child into school. Every lesson
she spoke good things about my art. Sometimes she asked
me about you. I said nothing. But she looked closely at my

paintings as if she searched for clues in them. I think she felt danger in my hand. Maybe danger in me.

Zak's mum tried too hard to make me speak of what I painted, to write an explanation in the notebook. She said I would get greater marks if I can talk about my work, but I told her, "I cannot place this art in words. It does not live in words."

One day she opened the art room door to a man I saw sometimes at the gates of school and once in Greenlands block visiting Kai. He wore uniform of a police officer kind. My teacher was expecting him. She nodded in my direction.

He came to sit on your empty seat at my side. When he told me he wanted to have "a little chat about Kai" I was in a panic thinking of what took place with your father. Questions flew from my mouth. "Is Kai OK? What is the matter? He has trouble?"

But the officer placed a calming hand on my shoulder. "No, no!" he said. "This is just a friendly, informal conversation. I'm fond of the lad and worried for his welfare. Your teacher told me you're special friends. You *are* friends, aren't you?"

I nodded. But I thought, why is he coming to me and not Orla or Zak who knew you all your life? I thought it is because they still do not trust me.

I told him I have not been close to you for some time. I think to myself I do not like to speak of my brother Kai behind your back so I didn't say anything else. I told this man I had to complete my painting for the art deadline. He stayed some time and looked at all my work. I hated him looking. I wanted to scream, *What have I done? Why do you not trust me? Because I am a refugee?*

I think he felt my silent anger because he stood, saying, "Thank you, Om. If you have anything else you want to say tell your teacher and she will come and find me."

On his way to the door I heard the conversation with Zak's mother. I tuned my ears in close, to hear more.

She was telling him, "I don't know, Yannis. I'm afraid Kai's falling through the cracks. He should be back in school. This is a tragedy unfolding." Tears were in her eyes.

After I heard this my hand and heart and eye were frozen. I could not concentrate because I thought to myself maybe I should have told this officer Yannis of these shadow boys visiting the Bothy. Every day I watched them take you far and far away but I could not say. I could not betray my brother.

There is one rule I learned on the road from despair. Only speak to those you will lay your life down to trust. I do not know many who are still alive. Only Aunt Gisou

and you and … in my hopes and in my fading dreams …
Ishy.

I wanted to tell my teacher, *Your name is Faith and you
named you daughter Hope. You must keep it for Kai. Let him
back in, this is the safest place for him.*

Later that day I painted wild flame after flame and in the
fire colours I was desperate to make someone understand
what it feels to be closed out, separate, to be no longer
welcome. You only leave when all hope is dead. All is
destroyed. This should not be for you, my brother Kai,
whose land is not destroyed.

"A slow start today, Om, but you've really caught the heat
in these flames. I can almost feel it coming off the paper."

"Yes! It is burning hot," I agreed, but I wanted to shout
at her, *You are his people. Fight for him.*

I was torn, for since the day your father tried to die I
felt the fear of trauma fire in me.

I thought if I told of what I saw in the Bothy, the shadow
boys on bikes, you would lose trust in me like you had lost
your trust in everybody. Your belief in me was the only
hope I had left for you.

So I kept my silence. And observed you beat-boxing with

raven birds in the shadow light of dusk and the drug cloud
rising from the Bothy. And that night I dreamed of fire.

Weak and shaking
when I woke,
I made a resolution walking into school.
I will paint your reflection.
I will show you with art.
I will draw you so you see yourself.
I will show you that you are not in pain alone.

This was my promise to you,
is my promise.
My brother Kai,
I will not let you burn.

Act 2

Raven Cries

Kai

The ravens have landed.
"Kai, Kai, Kai."

Squint through the broken blind
behind which
the ebony-winged birds shoot
shadow wings across my bedroom floor.

Open metal stash-tin.
What's left?
Just enough for a
cosh into sleep
tonight.

Don't smoke in the day.
That is what it always says
when it wakes.

Staggers up,
stares at the dishevelled face in the mirror.
Stubble shadow, sunken-eyed boy.

It takes a while to remember
this is me.

A knock at my bedroom door from far away. "Kai, love! Food's in the fridge... Back at eight. Get some fresh air. And try to keep out of Frankie's way. Oh and tidy up in there, will you, Kai? Everyone's got to play their part."

Dad's voice is in my ear.
"If I were a wise man, I would do my part.
Yet what I can I give him, give my heart."

Soft, melodious voice broken
with the one repeating note of
"Kai, Kai, Kai, Kai!"
Staring at me through the blinds,
my ravens have come for me.

"All right! Give it a rest. I'm awake! I'm awake!" I slide open the window and gulp a breath of ice-mist. Has it been one long winter since Sula died?

Squinting into the assault of morning, I listen for Orla moving around upstairs but her flat's silent. I stumble to the window and plant both hands against the frozen glass.

There's Orla sprinting up the road from the Rec. I watch

her power up the hill. She's changed.

Where have I been?
She slows to a stop now by Sula's tree,
raising her head to my balcony.
Does she still care enough to look for me?

"Kai, Kai, Kai," my ravens nudge.
"Shut up! Get out of my head! You can't talk!" I screech,
shooing them away.

What would she say if I tried to reach out to her now?
She jogs towards our block,
not looking up.
I shrink back inside.

"Kai, Kai, Kai, get yourself up and into school."
Even I know
it's the ravens, not Orla,
calling my name
over and over and over again.

"Stop messing with my head," I scream, sliding the door
closed,
locking it.

Clench fist,
driving into glass,
cringe at the pain.
Release at the shatter.

I watch the jagged zigzag grow.
Squawk, laugh, grawk,
Frankie will bust a gut.
Now I'm in trouble.

"Let us in, Kai. Let us in!"

One staring in,
tapping at my window now.
Open it up, just a crack.
It's all they need
and a raven swoops into my room.

"Come on now, Kai. Put your uniform on,
get back into school.
Clean yourself up."
It's the bossy one.

Now another comes strutting in.
"Don't let them shut you out.

If you've got to scream and shout to get back in
then do."

Maybe they're right.
I should put up more of a fight.

"Try, Kai, try."

I shake my head to loosen the haze.
It's lifting.
Kick a mouldy-smelling towel on the floor,
wrap it round my waist and wander to the bathroom,
shaking off the feeling I always get these days
whenever I step out of my bedroom ... that there is no place
for me here any more
without Dad.
In Mum's new "thank you, Frankie," sorted, settled, no-
drama life
that I think she likes.
If Dad ever comes home
will there be room for him here either?

Frankie's dust sheets over everything.
I search the living room. Every day that Dad's "away" –
that's what we say now,

"away" –
a different part of him is stowed into a box,
just till the paint's dry.
But it feels like it never will.
It never did in the Bothy.
I stare at the white box of our living room
and back through the open door to the squalor of my
bedroom,
the matted mound of this existence.

Wandering over to the shelf above the new TV
that Dad would hate,
I pick up the first photo of them with baby me.
All sunshine smiles. Real smiles, behind-the-eyes
smiles.
I look just like Dad did then.

I close the bathroom door, turn the hot tap on full,
twist the lid on the last drops of Dad's bath oil.
Sniff its woody scent.
I only mean to let a few drops in but my hand slips
and it empties.
Bubbles everywhere.
The overpowering scent of him
brings sudden wrenching sobs.

We're together again,
hacking our way through the wild.
Him telling stories,
singing to me.
Intoxicating,
head swirling.

This memory of happiness before
Sula,
before heaviness,
hopelessness.

I trace my fingers over my rib indents.
Is this my body?
Steam fills the bathroom,
cocooning vapour mist.
Dad's scent brings me home.

I dip my foot into the scalding water,
sense numbing.
Slowly immerse myself,
muscles untie,
chest opens,
mind meanders,
water overflows.

Curl limbs,
make myself Sula small.
Muffled sweet birdsong
from far away,
coming closer,
brighter,
dazzling me.
And into my eye
flies the skinny bird
fallen from its nest,
smashed on the ground
without a sound,
without a song,
blue sky is gone.

Water overflows.
Eyes sting.
Want to shout.
Climbing out.

Still wrapped in the towel, body steaming.
Heart thudding hard through skin,
lava flow rises from my stomach.
Salt tears breach
stinging cheeks.

Don't go there, Kai… Don't go…

"Keep your calm. Get to school and give it your best shot, mate."
Was that Dad's voice or the birds'? Or mine?
The ravens are outside — you can't hear them any more!
But then I feel them, inside, behind my eyes,
making them shine.
Hope wings batting against my chest,
spurring me on, spurring me on, spurring me on.
How are they doing this?
Following the walls, I reach for my stash,
just one more smoke to smooth the edges.
Nothing's going to stop me
walking through those gates…

Here they come again,
beating at my skin.
"*Kai, Kai, Kai, Kai, listen! You can trust us.*
We've got your back."
And in the dazzling shine of our eyes
ice-sun streaks through the broken window,
and I,
Kai, Kai, Kai,
finally
splinter.

I'm still going in but
I wish I hadn't come so early.
Got so out of it,
messed myself up.
Maybe I should go home,
bathe again
and try tomorrow...

Take a deep draw and pop the smoke out in satisfying
circles,
one,
two,
three...
Lie here in the wasteland,
squinting at the sky.

Bent double, rain-soaked,
eyes shielded against bright sun
blasting through grey.

Wringing out rain from matted hair,
uniform crumpled, smeared in mud,
shivering.

What's the point? What's the worth?
Hot tears blur vision, then through the mist an arc of colour
deepens,
conjuring, clearer now...
A rainbow in my eye.
Real or imagined? What does it matter?

Somewhere over the rainbow, bluebirds fly.
And the dream that you dare to.
Oh why, oh why can't I?

"Why can't I?
Why can't I?
Why can't I?"

I spy with my little eye Rain
of the broken eye,
and Bow
of the missing feathers.
Have they unbalanced your wings too?

Rain

They think they know us, Kai,
flock of unkindnesses,
not to be trusted,
stealers of shiny things, think we've no right to own.
Indigo-tinged,
black-winged,
iridescent.
Ill-omened,
screeching, gronking, squawking
harbingers of death.
Knife you in the back birds,
not to be trusted
black birds.
Shut them up,
shut them away,
shut them out.

Bow

Kicking around town,
clowning around,
can't they see us?
Hungry for knowledge,
loving, dancing, full-voiced,
loyal to our mates,
swooping towards truth.
Not too scared to stand up for ourselves.
Singing sweet so your heart swells,
playing magic tricks.
Beautiful,
tender-hearted
nurturers
never to be parted.
Flying across oceans,
dropping seeds,
building bridges.

Rain

Don't go on so, Bow.
The boy knows all that.
Just
never let them tell you
it doesn't hurt.
Sticks and stones
can break bones,
and words too
leave scars in the bricks and mortar,
poison the water.

Rave on
till they look us in the eye, Kai.
Surface cracked,
pain hatched.

Sometimes you've got to get up in their face.
Let them see
who's the real disgrace.

Bow

Cut it out, Rain.
We said we'd sing him a lullaby
not wind him up to rave on revolution.
Now look! Faith's passing by!
Hope's not dead, Kai.
You're just off your head
again.
Wake up now.
Get up, stand up
at the bars of the school gates.
Set that uniform straight,
don't be late.
Come on, Kai!
Wake yourself,
look sharp,
give it a shot.
Try, Kai, try.
Let them see the shine in our eye.
Go on! Stir yourself.
Find your words...

Kai

I pull myself up out of somewhere over a rainbow to hear sweet mum and daughter chatter skipping through the rain. It *is* Faith with her little Hope stabbing at my heart. I wait for them to say their goodbyes, like me and Sula didn't get a chance to, and walk towards Zak's mum. I'm unsteady on my feet and at the sight of me she's struggling to balance too.

I reach out to help with her bags but see the fear flash across her eyes and I back away.

"Please! Faith! Mrs Lawrence, I know I'm a mess today, but if I clean myself up can I come in tomorrow?"

My raven eye looks deep into hers as she takes in my muddied trousers and crumpled blazer.

Now she sniffs the air. "That's never going to happen if you turn up in this state, is it, Kai?"

"Please, Mrs Lawrence. Please don't turn your back..."

She cuts us off, flying towards the gates of Ravenscroft. But we fly faster, arm-wings stretched.

"What is it with these ravens?" She raises her umbrella to shoo them away.

"Sorry for everything..." Words slip from my mouth but

no one's listening. Zak's mum's not there. She's talking to someone on the phone. Calling for help.

Security guard steps forward, catching our wings as he bars the way. "On your way then, son. Look at the state of you!"

We panic-fly from his grasp.

Faith calls after us. "Sorry, Kai, I've tried but this is out of my hands."

Rain

Take my advice.
Refuse to be silent.
Fly higher, fly higher!
Storm the gates.
Don't let them clip your wings.
Can't fly under it,
can't fly over.
Wait till the mist begins to rise.
Then cut through, Kai.
Try.

Bow

Quieten yourself, Rain...
Can't you see the boy's in too much pain
to hear your fighting grawk?
Too bright is the shine of your one good eye.
Come now, Kai,
here's how it's done.
Brace, brace,
wingspan spread.
We all fall sometimes.
Pick yourself up,
try again.
Brace, brace,
that's the way.
Come, Kai.
Now you've got it.
That's the way.
Fly.
Fly, Kai, fly.

Rain

Raven revolutions.
Unclip our wings.
Fly with us, Kai.
Rave on revolutions.
What's to lose?

Brothers are dead.
Sister too.
So much pain in my head.
Let them go, Kai,
let them go.
Caw, caw, caw,
you're not alone any more.

Kai

Siren sounds,
stragglers race for the gate.
Alone
in the silence of our Rec

where the rainbow
has already faded...
What am I left with?
To scavenge in the undergrowth,
pecking at the leftovers.
What do I do on the Rec anyway?
Dance? Sing? Play? Pray?
Let arms float into wings,
hop along the path,
swerving fires and kicks.
Flapping,
tensing hands into claws,
hiding in the wilderness.
Burrow down into tear-sodden ground.
Peeking in through safety railings that cordon us off from
when we were chicks.

Back in the day
we used to spin and fly like Hope is now.
Rainbow swirling colours...
Fly low to see with my raven-eye view
the cracks under the smooth surface,
concrete ground, gashed sky smashed open.
Broken blue shell.
Descent into hell.

Where's left to fly now?
Split, split!
I scatter at the siren of Ravenscroft sounds.

Kai

"Thought we'd find you back here!" Taz doesn't bother knocking, just strolls right in like he owns the place, trying to take up more space than his skinny body holds. How did *he* get to be in charge when me and Zig are twice his size? Taz's skin is almost transparent. I eye the green veins at his temples he eyes my blazer as he takes a deep draw.

"Good shit, this stuff! Not still trying to break into that dump, are you?" He laughs, flicking the crest of my blazer. "Brought you some draw for looking after our wings!"

"I said I don't want stolen stuff in here," I mumble.

But Taz just hands me the smoke. Zig mumbles under his breath, "Take it, Kai. No use fighting it."

What wings has Taz clipped to make Zig so afraid?

Taz throws an arm round me, comradely. "Brother! You look rough. Why don't we ride out later?"

I shake my head, not even sure now if I could stand up.

My mind somersaults

                      through the high.

My belly too,

             held upside down in a rollercoaster.

Right way up again,
I'm steady enough to think I pity all three of us.
Is this all we have?
Roaming around after dark on stolen bikes?

"No, Taz. I don't want anything to do with your wheels. Can you get them out of here? I'm gonna stop smoking in the day. It's doing my head in. I just need it to help me sleep."

"We'll see!" he says but doesn't argue.

I stagger up and walk with them up the hill, past Sula's tree.

Whenever I'm here she makes me feel so guilty, like she's looking down on me.

"No worries, Kai... We'll see you right." I catch the shine in Taz's eye and it's not right. He grins at me.

I hear them ride away and with all Taz's big man acting I see how small and stringy he is. Zig, his muscle man, is as tall as me, stronger looking... Then it clicks. He's after me to be another Zig.

That's it, Kai.
Try, Kai, try.

These are not your brothers.
Find the fight in you.

I look up to the top balcony.
Where is Om?

Head clanging.
Metal door slamming.

Inside my empty flat,
inside my room,
slumped on my bed.
The ravens perched on the railings again.
I listen to their calls.

Their cries scale octaves.
Dad's sax in my head.
Temples throb,
but my mind is clear enough to remember
a halo of hope.
Was that me
this morning?
A lifetime ago,
lying in the bath.
Dreaming of cleaning up my act?

The ravens' cries siren through my mind.
I slide open the window,
lie on the floor.
They hop to my side,
one at each arm,
holding me in their wings.
Look to the shine in their eye, Kai.
Look to the shine in their eye.
I'm looking, Dad.

Bike wheels skid outside.

"Catch, mate!" Taz lobs up a package. "Nice one!" He laughs. "What's with the ravens on your shoulders? I know you said they're your mates but…"

"They are."

"Whatever, man. You've got *us* now. We look after our own. We'll stand by you. Look out for us later. We've got something else for you anyways, a bit of a thank you for joining our crew!"

Then my ravens go after him, chasing the shadows from my door. Taz flaps around, fending off Rain and Bow. "What's with these bloody black birds? What do they think they are, your bodyguards? Show them off, Zig."

They are my Greenland guardian angels,
I whisper under my breath.
We don't need you.
*I stand and watch them speed away as
the wind howls up the hill,
bending the boughs of Sula's tree.
So delicate those branches
and for a moment
I close my eyes and see myself speeding
away from everything here.
My heart is racing,
thudding against my chest bone
as I
slide the door closed
against the biting cold.
Huddle underneath my duvet,
desperate to sleep.*

*Know I won't get through without a smoke.
I clench the 'gift stash' in my palm,
unfurling frozen fingers.*

Orla

When I thought of you, which was pretty much all the time, I was desperate to do what I promised my mum I wouldn't and try to help. Especially the day of that bloody Greenlands Guardians meeting that was stressing me out. If anyone should have been there fighting to save this place it was you and your dad.

And if you couldn't or wouldn't I knew I had to show up, but I just felt so lonely. I was trying to sort out in my head what I would say to save our land, but all I could think of was you.

As I climbed the steps up to Om's flat I thought about how much had changed since he'd moved in. How now instead of me being his mentor I was the one leaning on him. I got why you were such good friends with Om. It's like he knows himself better than any of us do.

I buzzed at his intercom and after a while Om came to the door looking stressed out. Said he was sorry but he couldn't come after all because his aunt wasn't well. I asked him if she needed any help and then he said the strangest thing. "Only for me to stand by when shadows fall."

I stumbled back down with heavy legs. By the time I stood in that concrete hallway outside your door, I was crying floods for how alone I felt, for how much I wanted you by my side and for the memory of those days when we were flying and laughing and so full of life and sunshine.

Your mum came out of your flat, pulling a little case on wheels. She was surprised to see me there. I nodded at her but was about to hurry on because she hadn't even glanced at me since she called me a snake, but then she smiled and I realized I hadn't seen a light like that in her eyes in ages. "Orla love, I'm sorry for how I was. I shouldn't have taken it out on you."

"It's OK." I was wary but offered anyway, "If there's anything me and Mum can do..."

"There is actually!" Janice placed a hand on my arm. "I've left a note for Kai. He's fast asleep and I couldn't raise him." She rolled her eyes. "But if he surfaces tonight can you tell him that I've had a call to go and spend a couple of days with Dexter. The doctor thinks there's progress. Frankie's popping by to fix a window in Kai's room but..." She looked towards her door and sighed. "Keep half an eye out, Orlie? I think your mum's still got a spare key." And before I could answer she was gone into the dusk.

It really threw me. I felt sorry for your mum but I

saw red too, thinking how dare she put that on me! I leaned against the wall outside your flat for ages. Doubting myself because now I knew you were on your own I sensed this was my chance to come and talk to you. I thought, *What am I doing going off to a meeting?* Om's words kept racing through my mind. *Stand by when shadows fall...* Isn't that what I should be doing right now for Kai?

Then Zak texted to ask where I was because the councillor had already arrived and it was rude to keep him waiting. I wasn't thinking straight, feeling like the walls were closing in so I figured I wouldn't be any use to you anyway. I decided then that whatever happened I would go and see you in the morning and try to talk.

I was late and the light was already fading fast, but I had to see Sula's tree to remind me that this was our fight. While I stood there I felt it... That buried in the ground with all the sadness of her loss was also all the hope that had been placed in her. It was like how walking through our Greenlands made me see that everything we were doing to save this land was also about saving us, respecting out pasts and investing in our futures. And I knew what I needed to say and do.

I shone my phone torch, picked a leaf and placed it in my pocket, thinking I would give it to you and take a little piece of Sula with me to the meeting too.

I set a kind of test for myself, you know like we used to do as kids. If I can run up our Green Hill in less than a minute then I'll have good luck, that sort of thing. Even though I knew it was mad, I decided to walk through Greenlands in the dark... I suppose it was the closest thing I could get to walking with you.

It was eerily quiet as I felt my way from the frozen, spindly branches of Sula's tree with only my phone-torch as a guide.

Behind me, Om's balcony light switched on. *Did he do that for me?* As I turned back I lost my step and went careering down the path, sliding on my bum right to the Bothy, cursing myself because I'd dressed up smart to meet the councillor.

I was in a weird place that night, Kai, and the Bothy sort of drew me towards it, like I'd walked deep into a memory cave. I gagged as I pushed open the door because of the stink and then I saw those shadow boys leaning against our old camp bed, eyes rimmed red. Too stoned to hardly lift their heads. They shifted when they saw me.

"Hello, darlin'... Looking for a smoke? Come to join the party? Didn't know Kai brought his girl down here! Dirty little bastard. Well, what's his is ours, know what

I'm sayin', Zig?" He tried to grab me but his hands flailed around.

Sickened, I backed away. I'd seen enough: walls stacked up with shiny-looking brand-new bikes, and I felt sick at what you'd turned our Bothy into, Kai – a den for thieves and druggies. They came stumbling after me but relief flooded out fear as it was obvious they were too stoned to catch me as I scrambled round the side of the Bothy on my hands and knees, following the school railings.

I got a stick and beat my way through, wishing I could run far away from Greenlands and all its shadows. I felt it then, what before had made no sense to me, the thing your dad said about wings being unbalanced... The last place in the world I wanted to step into that night was Zak's cosy life. Just then I got how you resented him but mostly it was you I resented … for making it so hard to help you.

By the time I arrived at Zak's door, I was scratched up and covered in mud. I nearly fell into Zak when he opened the door.

Faith came through, took one look at me and held me in her arms. "Oh, Orla! Whatever's happened? I thought you were coming with your mum. No Gisou and Om?"

"They couldn't make it but I'm fine. I took a short cut through Greenlands for inspiration but I … fell over. Can I borrow some clean clothes? Tell them I'll be ready to speak in ten minutes."

Faith breathed a sigh of relief and didn't ask me any more questions though I could tell she was holding back. "Zak, you go and hold the fort," she ordered. "I'll help Orla find a towel for a shower and some clothes."

I had never had a shower like that in my life – ours is a trickle. That hot, steamy water helped to blast away some of the heaviness in my heart. I could have stayed in there for hours, pampering myself with Faith's sweet-scented oils and soap. For a moment I almost forgot I had a job to do.

I quickly dried myself and slung on the sweatshirt and joggers that Faith had laid out for me and, as I scooped my dirty clothes into a plastic bag, the leaf from Sula's tree fluttered out. I picked it up as I passed Hope's bedroom and clenched it tightly in my palm.

When I walked into the living room the table was covered in documents and papers. Faith had left a place beside her at the head of the table and there were empty spaces along the benches for Mum, Gisou and Om. I felt like we'd let her down. I explained that they all sent their apologies. I didn't tell her that I never actually invited my mum because I got it in my head that there was no way I wanted her to go to Zak's house. Don't get me wrong: I'm not ashamed of how we live. It was the way that Zak's mum and dad insisted on me calling them Faith and Joel and treated me like their daughter. I thought Mum would hate that, although I knew she would have been proud to see that I was taking a lead in the campaign.

Faith smiled reassuringly. I respected how she'd taken me under her wing despite it being obvious that things were tense between me and Zak. Even so, I felt this rage rise up in me towards everyone sitting round the table, even her. I saw it how it was. For them saving the Rec and our little patch of Greenlands wood felt like some kind of community exercise. If they lost what would it really mean to any of them? I turned to Zak and scowled, remembering how his first thought about losing the Rec was wondering where he'd play footie.

There was one new person at the table and it took me a while to recognize him out of uniform. It was the Community Police Officer from school – Yannis. After what I'd just seen in the Bothy him being there didn't make it any easier. "I thought you said the councillor was here!" I whispered.

"Yannis is the new councillor!" Zak explained, doing his foot-tapping tick. He kept glancing at me, not sure any more how to read me or maybe he could tell I was about to blow. His dad was talking on and on about how he could write an article and get the press involved. I only vaguely registered what they were droning on about. Now they were working through their agenda: trees, bats, woodland, planning regulations, access, parking, pollution, ravens and residents' rights... That was the order the agenda was written in. It made me want to get up and leave. But there I was, taking the minutes.

Someone was saying, "Our best bet might be the bat report," and I wrote that down, wondering if I was stuck in some alternative reality. It was like I was looking down on myself in the soft haze of that lamplit room and suddenly I just knew that it was so wrong that this meeting was here and not in Greenlands.

"So far I think the council have been quite amenable," Yannis said and read out their answers to our objections. The council had given reassurances that:

- **The walkways and access to the schools through the Rec will not be compromised.**
- **A section of the Rec will be retained for recreation purposes from which both adjacent schools can benefit.**
- **The "access route/road" to the three planned housing blocks with attendant parking can be adjusted to avoid damage to ancient trees and wildlife.**

"Orla, would you like to tell the councillor what you planned to say?" I stared back at Faith blankly so she prompted me again. "Orla has prepared a speech on behalf of the residents of Greenlands flats." Faith smiled at me expectantly and all the words I'd been rehearsing on the way scattered in my brain. I unfurled my left hand and held the crushed leaf up to them.

"What about Sula's tree?" That one question just tore out because losing Sula was always right in front of me when I was fighting for the Rec, like a beacon.

Faith laid a comforting hand on my arm and I thought about little Hope upstairs all tucked up in her cosy bed. I saw the pain in Faith's eyes too and I knew she felt the unfairness of it all so I thawed out a bit.

But then came the last two points on the agenda.

"Complaint report of delinquent and criminal activity in woodland. Risk assessment of criminal activity."

When Zak's dad read this out I could feel Yannis watching me closely. All I could think of was how much trouble you could be in. And, just when I thought it couldn't get any worse, Joel mentioned to Yannis that his brand-new bike had been stolen and I felt like I was going to crack.

Yannis nodded. "Yours is the eighteenth bike stolen in the past month. Almost certainly connected to a group of excluded youths who've moved into the area. We had a complaint from a resident who was almost knocked over the other day by a boy riding down the road with no lights.

If we're going to make any headway we need to make sure that there is no more criminal activity around Greenlands." Yannis looked straight at me when he said that. "I'm afraid I have to go now. Send me the minutes and I'll keep trying to advocate on the community's behalf. I live here too, you know."

Once he was gone there was some chatter about how lucky we were to have him onside. And then there was the flint that set me off... I don't know who said it but I can remember the words. "Now about the name – Greenlands Guardians. Could we find something more ... catchy to ramp up the level of local support we need from the whole area? And maybe change the logo? I know Om's ravens are supposed to look like guardians but some people find ravens a bit menacing. It could put people off..."

Suddenly I was smouldering on Om's behalf. What used to be ours was being taken over, even the name you thought up. It was yours and your dad's discovery. You were the original guardians. Now everything was being taken away and I was the only one here from Greenlands with a say.

I looked round Zak's walls covered in bright paintings and posters, bookshelves bowing under their weight, and a force rose up out of my belly. I suppose it was confidence of a kind.

I just couldn't listen to their talk, talk, talk any more.

I scraped my chair back, kicked it away and heard it crash to the floor behind me. Faith was on her feet too, concern in her eyes as I lashed out. "You can't even save a boy when he stands outside the gate of your school and cries for you to let him in. You just watch him slipping away and you walk on by and, and…" I couldn't speak another word I was so choked.

Around me there was whispering. Faith and Joel broke the meeting up. Faith kept trying to sit me down to talk, reminding me that she had tried everything, but I was having none of it. In the end Joel told Zak to walk me home, ignoring my protests that I *wanted* to walk back on my own.

At the door Faith said she understood how angry I was but it was a shame I hadn't been able to contain myself for the meeting. I couldn't, Kai. All I wanted at that moment was to turn back time to the day I spun you on the swing, in a spell of sunshine. All I wanted was to spin us back to that time when me, you and Zak were playing in our den and everything felt innocent.

Zak and I walked on in silence. Past the entrance to the school walkway imprinted with our memories. Primary and secondary… It felt like we were walking through our lives that night. So bitter cold you could feel the stillness. The quiet rang in my ears like an alarm.

You know I've never been a fan of your ravens but it was strange not to see or hear them.

Zak kept trying to get me to talk. He offered me his coat but I shrugged him off. He asked again and again, "Do you know what's going on with Kai? Just tell me! What can I do?"

"You think I'm going to tell *you*! Because of you he's out of school," I finally snapped.

The only one I wanted then was you, Kai, and Zak knew it. I was all torn apart. I thought about love… Different kinds of love, brother and sister love, love for Sula buried under a tree before her life even started, your love for your dad whose mind had flown, love that burns you inside out. Yes, Kai. I'm talking about love for you. I didn't know the ways that you could love back then but I have always loved you, even if not in the way you wanted me to. What you were doing to yourself and us was breaking my heart.

Outside our flat Zak tried to hold me but I pulled away and I didn't say what I wanted to. When we were little it really did feel that we were equal. Friends forever that nothing and no one could ever break apart. But it wasn't true at that moment. I turned away from Zak and slammed the metal door behind me without saying anything, not a word, and we both knew whatever had been between me and him was over.

When I finally calmed down I realized I should wait till morning to talk to you.

But even in my sleep I saw flames and shadows. You disappearing into smoke and the ravens coming as messengers, screeching at me to find the key.

That night was the first time I had the nightmare that's haunted me many times since. See, Kai! You weren't the only one to feel those foreshadowings.

It was just getting light when I woke up, knowing that I had to see you, to speak to you then and there. Find a way to get through, to clear up the mess. In the dark I opened the balcony door and heard you clattering around below, like you were wrecking the place. I supposed you were off your head as usual. I closed the door, plugged in my headphones and remembered the key in my dream and what Janice said, about us having a spare. The last thing I thought before I finally got back to sleep, wondering what sort of state you were in, was: *If you won't answer the door I'll find the key and let myself in.*

Kai

I wake to the sound of pecking on the broken pane. Bow's outside the window, squawking. I was sure they slept in here last night but maybe I let them out. If Mum found them and had to release them I'd be in deep trouble.

"Sleeping like a baby you were! We let ourselves in – just slid that balcony door of yours open. Easy!"

I bash my hands against my temples. Not this again.

I raise my head off the pillow and that's when I know it's worse than ravens in my mind. Taz is standing in the bedroom doorway with Zig at his shoulder.

"Wasn't expecting those ravens of yours to come attacking us though."

I stare from Taz to Zig, heart thudding, shivering, not able to take any of this in.

"Saw your mummy leaving so we thought it was about time we paid you a home visit!" Taz is holding a note. "Gone to see your dad, so we have the place to ourselves for two whole days!"

My chest is on fire. I stagger out of my bedroom to see him making himself comfortable at the kitchen table.

"Thoughtful of you to get the beers in!" Taz laughs, downing a glug of the beer.

"What do you want from me?" I snap.

Taz moves to Dad's chair where no one has sat since that day he went away. Mum won't even let Frankie sit there. Now he puts his filthy feet on the table and pats the cushion on Mum's chair for me to come and join him. Zig hangs back, shifting from foot to foot. I don't move so Taz gives Zig the nod and he steers me to sit.

"Had a little visit from your pretty little girlfriend upstairs!"

"She's not…"

Taz puts his finger to my lips. "Did I ask you to speak? Thing is, Kai, we've been thinking how generous we've been and we haven't finished with you yet. This is the best set of wings we've ever laid our hands on –" he spins the wheel of a bike discarded on the floor – "and it's for you. All you have to do is look after our little store and make sure your girlfriend doesn't breathe a word about the bikes." Taz takes a sharp little knife out of his pocket. "Unless she wants to feel a bit of blade!"

I feel sick. "Leave her alone!"

"Just tell her we know where to find her if she squeaks! She did us a favour, as it happens. Got us thinking about security. We bought you a padlock so you can look after the wheels we've moved in. You've got a proper bird's-eye view from here." Taz sneers at me. "And we know how you love your birds! The perfect little lock-up that – just tell your girlfriend and your old mates to steer clear."

I stand suddenly, head spinning. "I told you, Taz, I don't want anything to do with the bikes... I'm not into this. Take them back and this one too. I don't want—"

"Nah, see, it's not as easy as that, mate."

Zig stands behind me, lays both hands on my shoulders and pushes me back down.

I hear my heart bellow, and I hardly recognize the words that scratch at my throat. "Get out, get out!" I hurl at them with the shrill alarm of ravens warning.

Taz slides a bottle of beer over to me. "What the hell! Keep your voice down. You've spent too long knocking around with those birds."

Fly, Kai, fly.
Try, Kai, try.
Fly, Kai, fly!

"What did it say?" Taz asks, teeth clenched, menacing now.

"Come on, Taz! He's not right in the head. Let's go before he loses it completely. What if someone hears?" Zig gathers up his things, but Taz holds my gaze steady and straight, taking another leisurely swig of beer.

"You see, Kai, this is how it is now. Didn't want to have to spell it out but you don't seem to get the deal. We put our trust in you and you owe us. We want to ... prove that we're *always* here for you. You're our brother now, Kai, and we never let our fam down."

"No, Taz!"

Zig steps forward to shield me but he's too late. I see the flint in Taz's eyes and he's coming at me.

I gag at the contact of heavy metal on forehead.
Blood spurts,
eye throbs
at the force of the blow
sending me stumbling backwards
over the metal body of the bike.
Light fades.
Zig in the distance pleading with Taz to stop.
"Come on, Taz, that's enough — you've shown him who's boss. Let's get out of here."

Taz looms above me, holding my wrist and twisting hard. My mind flickers again and next thing I'm on the floor, his feet planted either side of me. Then his knees drop hard and heavy into my sternum. A gasp of crushed breath shoots out.

"So? You with us?"

I shake my head. Blood trickles into my eye.

"A little sharp shock should do the job!" The flash of his penknife at my eye. "Now we can't have you letting your ravens in and not us, can we? We've got a reputation to keep up." Taz leans forward, face-to-face with me now, the blade protruding from between the fingers of his clenched fist. In a flash I see Dad on the roof, his arms outstretched like raven wings. I feel something inside me fall, dislodge, and I'm spiralling into the eye of a storm.

I am nothing more than my eyes,
braced, charged.
Taz's blade is grafted on to him,
a cat's claw
leaning in.
Beer breath, weed and venom
seep from him.
Voices a blur.
Hand stuffing mouth,
petrol fumes.
Chest heaves,

hands hold me
down,
down,
down.
Eyes stare into eyes.
Hesitation, fear, panic rise.

"Come on, Taz! We've done enough to scare him.
He won't blow us out again!"

"Shut it, Zig. *I* say when we've done enough!"

Eyes open,
searching for kindness.
Am I afraid?
My heart holds constant now,
every beat, deafeningly loud,
pounds
in my chest cavity and in my ears,
at my temples.
Has the blade cut me?
My body's a hollow cave.
Home to a drumming heart, still beating.
Still breathing.
How long will it take, if the blade hits an artery,
for me to bleed to death?

"Right! Scalp time!" Taz smooths his hand over my head and points to Zig. "Got to look sharp." He flicks through the blades of his knife and tests the edge of one. I hold my breath as a soft foam covers my head, then he grabs at my hair and I feel the sting of part of me coming away – I don't know if it's hair or skin.

Shave after shave after shave.

Looking into Taz's eyes, I am hypnotized by the concentration on his face.

He holds me in his grip for ages, like a surgeon taking pride in his work. Taz raises my hand to my head so I can feel. "Not a bad shave that, as it goes. Just a few nicks here and there!"

"Zig! What's our number-one rule?" Taz asks, casting around showman-style. I struggle to lever myself on to my elbows but Zig's holding me down. Blood trickles into my mouth from above my eye and my head floats.

"Never take back wings."

"That's right. Listen to Zig here – he knows the score."

Now Taz pulls up my fleece and I feel the cool air on my skin as he jabs the knife towards my heart.

Is it true that when you're stabbed too deep you don't feel pain? I am a single-cell amoeba, my only function now a pulse.

"Turn over, mate. This won't hurt ... much!" Taz shoves

my shoulder and I feel a foot in the flat of my back and
a blade piercing my skin over and over... I close my eyes
against the pain.

Rain's somewhere high above me,
I think,
or inside.
I feel his shadow wings
fluttering in my chest.
Not Rain but Dad's voice.
Look to the shine in their eye,
Kai.
You know what you have to do, my son.
Unclip your wings
and all will be well again.
Don't cry.
Fly, Kai,
fly...

Down, down, down I fall between broken shards of dust,
stone, brick, blood, bone.
Shadow wings of Rain
soar through an ancient tower to the floor.
Goodbye, Kai, goodbye.
Where's Bow?

Not her time yet or yours.
Don't cry, Kai.
Somewhere over the rainbow,
Dad's lullaby notes
soothing Sula and me,
I drift away.

Eyelids open.

"Thanks for the hospitality." Taz holds up bloodied hands. "While you were sleeping like a baby we left another little present on the balcony for you. Reckon we've done you a favour. Zig's been down and locked up, save you the bother tonight." He sniffs the air. "Had a bit of a shifty smoke, did you, Zig?"

"Just a quickie."

Taz shoves some keys in my palm, forcing my fingers to close round them. As I pull away he twists my swollen wrist. I moan with pain.

"A set of keys for you and we've got one too. Shared ownership we'll call it. Just make sure your little friends get the message to keep their noses out or we'll be paying them a visit too!"

He pats my shorn head like I'm his dog. "Good boy. All clean-shaved now. Smooth as a newborn."

Orla

I held on to Sula's leaf all that night and I woke to a fresh pine smell and a new light outside my window ... snow-light. I opened the balcony door to the first dusting, thinking I would go for a run and get my head straight before I came to see you.

But the insistent alarm of a single raven got right under my skin. Then, looking down, I saw blood spattered in the snow below.

The call of the raven morphed in my mind and seemed to be calling your name. "Kai, Kai, Kai, Kai, Kai."

"Keep half an eye out, Orlie?" Janice's words played through my head. I heard your door open and relief washed over me...

"Are you were OK, Kai?" I called out, but just as quickly the door closed again and then there was silence. I didn't see the raven fly away and I couldn't work it out but then it dawned on me – you must have let it in.

I ran to the drawer where Mum keeps all the keys and found yours at the back with the crown key ring still attached. I grabbed it and sprinted down the stairs. Rang on the intercom, knocked a few times and waited but heard nothing except a raven cawing inside.

I let myself in. The smell of beer and blood hit me and I actually gagged at the state of the place. Your flat was covered in filth from bike wheels, boot treads, spatters of blood speckling the walls and floor. Bottles of beer were strewn across every surface. A silver bike was propped against the sofa. I thought I'd seen the bike before ... Joel's bike. I just couldn't believe what I was seeing. In the middle of one of the cushions there was something like a nest but when I looked closer I saw it was coils of hair...

I picked them up and felt them between my fingers – your hair, Kai. Your beautiful lush, thick curls, all shorn.

"Kai?" My voice, strangled by fear, hardly surfaced. By then I was terrified.

Still no answer came from your bedroom. Now I felt for my phone because I was really frightened of what I would find. I took a deep breath, opened your door and stepped inside.

Relief flooded through me when I found you sitting on your bed, hardly recognizable with your hair shaved, all scabbed and bloodied. You stared at me with vacant eyes, a raven by your side and bloodstains over your hands, face and covers. If I had passed you on the street, I would not have known you, Kai. Your eyes sunk deep into red and purple rings and your bloodstained face contorted in sadness.

I shivered, scanning the room. It was freezing. I edged my way round the wall with the idea to let the raven out and close the windows tight shut but the bird stood firm, making this strange gurgling sound. I picked my way across the upturned furniture, stepping over piles of clothes, books, putrid yellow liquid stains and droppings. I closed my nostrils against the stench of rot and pushed on through to the balcony, hoping the raven would fly from your side but it refused to budge.

"Orla! Don't shut her out. She's lost her Rain, nowhere to go." Tears began to flow down your blood-streaked cheeks.

"OK, OK…" I soothed, leaving the door open.

"Orlie, never, ever go back to the Bothy. Promise me. Tell Om too."

Then you started making the same gurgling, clicking noise as the raven. "OK, but Kai, what have you done to yourself?" I tentatively walked towards you and the raven. You stared at me with a dazed expression that made me more afraid than anything. Like you had flown somewhere else. You were shivering violently and whimpering. I followed the blood smear over your forehead down your arms to your hands and saw that one wrist was out of shape and cupped at a strange angle. You flinched away as I reached out, as if

I were trying to steal something precious from you.

"Broken wing and broken eye," you kept muttering under your breath.

But then something else caught my attention. Feathers protruded between the fingers of your good hand and I gently coaxed them open. It was all I could do not to retch at what I found – a raven's body smashed to a pulp in your bloody palm.

"Don't fear the ravens, Kai. Look to the shine in their eye." You kept saying that. I gently eased apart the fingers of your hurt hand, blocking out your moans. I had to see … and there in a pool of ruby-red blood was what I feared: the severed head of one of your precious ravens.

I leaned over the balcony and retched and retched and retched.

"Piece it together again, Orlie, can you?" you asked, rocking backwards and forwards as you nursed the bird on your lap as if it were a baby.

"What happened, Kai?"

"Blue sky's broken, Orlie. Rain is dead. They say I have to take their wings, but I don't want to."

It was so strange, like we were children again, playing some macabre game – but this was too real. I could hardly see through my tears but I hunted around the mess of your room to find an old trainer box, lined it with a T-shirt and gently prised the bird from your hand. You did not resist as I wrapped the head inside, gagging at the sweet, thick smell of cloying blood.

"Let's clean these wounds." I eased you to your feet but you moved your limbs like you were sleepwalking as we walked together to the bathroom.

I slowly undressed you, gently peeling the bloodied fleece from your skin. Not knowing what I'd find. If you could do this to your home ... then what could you do to yourself?

Your belly was scored with raw, shallow cuts in rusty-coloured shapes that looked like wheels and wings. I had seen marks like that before, graffitied on the Bothy walls. I held my breath as I checked each one to find that none of them were scored too deep. You were naked now, Kai, ribs and hip bones protruding through your skin. You leaned heavily against me as you climbed into the bath. The surviving raven flew up to the shower railing, peering down at us. I shuddered at its intense gaze.

I let the water flow over your head and face to rinse the blood away. You winced at the sting and smart of the water on your skin. I thought, *How has beautiful, brave, talented Kai come to this?*

Great sobs racked my body. I knew I could not leave you alone. Not for a second. Needing to be closer,

I climbed over the bath rim and let the hot water wash over both of us. My clothes ballooned as you curled your limbs into a foetal position, and laid your head on my chest. I cupped water in my hands and poured it over the gash on your forehead, until all the blood was cleaned away.

It seemed to me that there had been a vile ritual ceremony, with the raven as some kind of sacrifice. But I knew I had to clean you up and maybe try to clear the flat before I called for help. I don't know why my pride and yours felt so closely linked, but I couldn't stand to let anyone else see you like that, mired in filth.

I got out, stripped off my own wet clothes, grabbed a dressing gown for myself and wrapped you in a towel.

I shuddered to think that I had closed my mind and eyes to what had been happening to you all this time, only a floor away from me. Now you were calmer, I told you I had to go for help, but you clung on to me like you would never let go. You spoke the strangest words of all then.

"I should have warned them
when the song thrush fell
before her wings were grown.
I should have warned them."

I carefully lifted up the shoebox containing the dead raven but the living one started kicking up such a fuss, wings bashing against my arm, that I dropped the box back on the bed.

"Bow, Orlie's our friend – she won't hurt us," you reassured the raven, picking up the coffin-box and clinging on to it. "Orlie, can you hold me? Wrap me in sunshine?" And you pulled out Sula's blanket from under your pillow. So I wrapped it round you.

I couldn't stand the pain of seeing you like this and I found myself climbing in beside you. Loading covers over both of us against the chill air seeping through the window.

"Bring Bow too," you whispered and the raven came hopping on to your bed.

You closed your eyes, stretched out a hand to me and whispered, "I love you, Orlie."

The words were so soft and quiet I thought I might have imagined them. My eyes stung hot. I heard your breathing change as if you were about to sleep and then I remembered my first-aid training. "You've hurt your head, Kai. Try to stay awake while I go for help," but you'd wrapped yourself round me, your limbs entangled in mine and Sula's sunshine blanket.

Just wait till he relaxes then go for help, I told myself. But every time I tried to shift you lifted your good hand to touch my face, tracing your fingers over my eyes and cheeks and down to my mouth as if to work out whether I was real.

"Are you an angel?" you whispered. I shook my head but, remembering the leaf from Sula's tree, I placed it in your hand.

Then I held you, smoothing my fingers over your temples. I stared into the raven's eyes as if it could show me what I had to do, and, as I did, my own eyes grew heavy.

Bow

You see,
they have beheaded Rain
and they will take your head too.
You must go, son.
We cannot be free,
you and me,
until we set the ravens free.
Remember, Kai,
a trapped bird cannot sing.
Don't let them steal your music.
Fly, Kai,
fly.

Act 3

Fly, Kai, Fly

Omid

There is more than one way to tell. Sit with me beside this Sula tree and I will try to speak for you in art, as your brother. With your sister spirit beside us. It is my gift.

One day you may be able to give these pictures, the story of this time, more words, but for now these will serve. The feeling of starting to communicate is like water finding its way through hard rock... If it surfaces it will find a place to flow more freely, if not now then someday.

Now I speak with my Omid eye. I do for you what I do for myself: listen close and sketch and sketch until the image I plant on the page brings something of the story back.

Orla

I opened my eyes, shooting up off my pillow, disorientated, racking my mind to remember where I was. "Kai?" I whispered, wildly casting around for you.

How could I have fallen asleep?

My heart pounded in panic as I took in the bloodied, filthy state of where we had slept in the wretched mess of the night before. I registered my mum's voice screaming in my ear and the shock on her face as she entered the chaos of your flat to find me standing in the middle of it, wearing nothing but a dressing gown.

And here was Frankie too, shouting at me. Hunting round the flat, calling your name, demanding to know, shaking me out of my stupor. "Where is he, Orla?"

I looked from the open window where the living raven perched to the empty bed. "He's gone!" I said.

"Get her out of here, Holly. I'll evacuate the building," Frankie ordered.

I felt my mum's arms round me, her coat over my shoulders. Someone put my shoes on and walked me out of your flat. The stench of smoke entered my nostrils at the same time as I saw it pluming into the sky and I froze in horror at the sight of our Bothy ablaze. Lights flashing on the roads, sirens blaring. The raven you called Bow circled round and round Sula's tree as if protecting it.

My mum's voice came to me. "Orla, I thought you were down there in the fire." She grabbed me and held me in her arms, so tight I could hardly breathe. Then came the barrage of questions but I was numb with cold and shock.

Frankie came out of Greenlands, helping Om walk with

his Aunt Gisou. Her face was covered with a shawl like she couldn't stand to see. I saw her shaking violently and read the fearful question in Om's eye. "Where's Kai?" he whispered, staring at the Bothy.

"You think he could be down there?" Frankie asked, forcing me to face him. "Orla, what sort of state was he in when you saw him?"

Splintered words tore out of me. "Desperate... I saw others in there too yesterday. From that gang, smoking." Then Frankie was gone, shouting to the other firefighters that there could be a child in there.

And that word "child" broke me because we were still children then and none of this should ever have happened.

I cannot leave my Rain
but your
wheels are wings
so fly, Kai, fly.

Omid

When she saw the fire my aunt fell to the floor.
She was in panic, trauma-fear, curled up on the
pavement. Making shields of her hands, hiding from
fire-memory. Underneath her covers she was chanting.
"No more death, no more dying... No more burning,
no more destruction, no more crying..."

Wind is still high
but here I lie,
silent and alone
with stolen wings,
broken claws
clinging on.
Heading
into the broken, bloodied eye
of the storm.

Orla

Om's Aunt Gisou was seriously distressed. She was leaning heavily on Om and crying. "This is not the first time we have fled from fire," Om explained to Frankie. "It brings memory – flames too close."

When we were all safely out I heard Frankie call Janice and tell her to come home. You were wrong about him, Kai. I don't think he was moving in on your mum. I know it's hard for you to believe it, but I think he was just doing out of uniform what he does for work. He wants to save people. The way he spoke to your mum so gentle and kind, asking after your dad too. Telling her to come home and to let him know when she was close. It didn't sound like anything but friendship to me.

Yannis arrived and he took me and Om aside and begged us to tell him all the details, everything we knew.

"Kai was down there this morning, kneeling in the mud when I laid out my mat to pray. It was dawn," Om told him.

"And you stayed in his flat overnight?" Yannis asked me gently. "Is that right, Orla?"

"He... He was in a terrible way. I think he's really ill.

I found him with a beheaded raven in his hands. Like he'd been involved in some sort of ritual," I managed to say, but I felt like my mouth and body were disconnected.

By then the stench of fumes and blackened air began to engulf Greenlands wood. Flames tore out of the Bothy window and we kept getting pushed further back. A cordon was set up and as I watched in horror I knew for sure that if you were in there you were burning.

I heard a dragging sound as a heavy hose was hauled down the hill, urgent voices calling, instructing, ordering. "Get some grit on these paths. Set up another cordon further back. That fire's going to take some putting out. Petrol, I think. Let's have this blaze out before it sets the whole wood alight."

Om laid his coat on the ground beside me, lowering his head to the earth and rising, and even though I've never prayed in my whole life I took his hand and kneeled beside him.

Bow whipped up a wing storm above Sula's tree, shrieking and shrieking and refusing to fly away from the rising flames. That's what made me think you were in there and all hope of you being alive ebbed from me. I have never felt that cold.

I was taken into the ambulance and someone wrapped a silver cloak round my shaking body. I let Mum cradle me on her lap. Beside us was Om's aunt who touched my cheek and clasped Om's hand. Then I cried like I haven't cried since I was a baby. *This is my fault... If I had gone for help...*

Once I was warmer the police helped me and Mum into one car and Om and his Aunt Gisou into another.

Slowly we moved through the gathering crowds. Flashes of illuminated faces caught in the siren light.

The police officer spoke constantly under his breath into his intercom as he drove, his colleague making notes. "Two sixteen-year-olds from Greenlands estate. Evidence of mental-health crisis. Record of last visiting boy's father at this address – attempted suicide. Blood on site in the flat. Evidence of drug taking... Possibly three unaccounted for. Forensics at work."

"He must have gone to bury the raven down there," I told Mum, but she hushed me, saying I could tell everything to the police when we gave evidence.

"Kai's mother has been informed and is on her way home." The police officer turned round to reassure us.

I looked out of the window to the street lights reflecting off the deepening snow, trying my hardest to push the picture from my mind of Janice walking back into the wreckage of Greenlands. Just then I saw someone slink back behind a hedge. I peered closer. It was definitely one of the shaven-headed boys I'd seen in the Bothy. Not the one that leered at me, the other. He caught my eye and I read guilt and a glint of recognition in his eyes too.

"Stop! He was there! In the Bothy yesterday! You should question him, and his sidekick. Kai was hanging out with them. Look at his head, shaved too. Kai loved his hair – he would never do that to himself." I suppose I wasn't making much sense but I was sure the shadow boy must have known something.

The police car slowed and reversed, pulling up on the kerb. The officer got out and walked over to the boy. He was shivering and as he spoke to the policewoman he broke down in tears, pointing over to the Bothy where thick smoke poured over Greenlands.

The officer took a firm hold of the boy's arm and leaned into the car. "I've called for backup. I'm bringing him in. He was in there, smoking. You go ahead with these two."

"Have you seen Kai? He wasn't in there, was he?" I shouted through the window, but before he could answer we moved off.

I couldn't help but stare at the boy's neck tattoo. The tag on the walls of the Bothy and the tag on his skin was the same one that you had on your body.

"How could I be so stupid?" I shot forward in my seat. "He couldn't have tattooed himself, could he? It was them! It must have been them in his flat... Last night there was a bike, Joel's bike, and it was gone this morning!"

"Calm yourself, Miss. We'll take a full statement when we get to the station," the police officer said, and I saw the look of pity in his eyes too. He let out a deep sigh as he read a message on his phone. "No one was found in the burning building. Nothing except bikes."

And slowly, as we drove through town, I began to breathe again. Me and Mum held each other close and I watched the snow drift and cover the ground. I thought that if we could all be together again we could print ourselves in this perfect carpeted earth and start all over again.

At the station my head pounded with all the questions.

"So you stayed the night in Kai's flat?"

"Was there a party?"

"What is the nature of your relationship with Kai?"

"The flat has been ransacked."

"And you definitely recognized the bike?"

"How many bikes did you see in the shed you call the Bothy?"

"Is it possible that Kai wrecked his own flat?"

"Tell us about the boys he was hanging out with. Could you identify the other boy?"

But the question that was hardest to answer was,

"Why didn't you alert your mother or anyone else to the state that Kai was in, knowing that his father had attempted suicide?"

That's haunted me ever since. If I could turn back the clock and change what I did that night... I stayed out of love and protection for you, because I couldn't stand to let anyone else see you like that, but I know now I was wrong. I wasted time. Zak wasn't a snake when he told his mum he was afraid for you... He was brave and I was the coward. I could have saved you from a whole world of pain.

Watching ice breath
and the drift of snow,
I sang and sang
a song I remembered.
A song of bleak
midwinter.

Omid

The police kept asking me about our art. In the wreck of
the Bothy they found pieces of wall plaster with traces of
our paintings on. I asked if I could keep them because
they held pieces of me but they did not answer me.
They stopped the interview and told me I must wait.

My aunt became upset, saying we must have a lawyer
and also a translator. After a long time both came and
they interviewed me again. I felt the shadows fall in me,
remembering all those times before when we had to answer so
many questions from cold eyes, as if we had done something
wrong, instead of all the wrong done to us. My aunt sat by
my side, hand held tight in mine. She became upset more
than once asking the translator if they suspected me, saying,
"Omid was this boy's good friend. Why do they always think
the worst of us?" I tried to calm her.

I explained again about the art at school – that I
made it so Kai would have an opportunity to see himself.
They asked me why I painted many flames and fires.
I spoke in Arabic to the translator so that my aunt could
fully understand too. "Because there are fires in my heart.
Because my home, my family and all I know was burned.

But fires burn everywhere… Maybe I can see them more than these people."

The translator did not repeat all I said, only saying, "Omid sees his work as a way to express the trauma he has lived through. He thought showing his friend how to do it might help him too."

I saw in one of the officer's eyes that he does not trust me. "I'm struggling with this, Omid. I'm not sure I understand how you think drawings and paintings of fires can save people?"

Then they stopped the interview and brought a child psychiatrist to see me. I became angry. I said I am not a child, I know my mind. But I was starting to doubt myself. I was thinking perhaps there was too much truth in my art. Maybe, in trying to help Kai, I hurt him more.

I tried to explain again. Told the psychiatrist that I painted with Kai in the Bothy because we both needed to get feelings out. When I came here I understood that I had things to show Kai. I have seen many people lost in their minds, like his father. And I have seen it many times that, though you may think that there will be no new paths, the pain can soften. For I know what it is to be lost. I have some experience.

In the end they accepted the statement and offered to drive me and Aunt Gisou

home in a police car, but she refused. Instead we waited in the
snow for a bus. Her face was stone. She said only one thing.
"I warned you, Omid, that this boy would bring shadows to our
door. Now all we can do is pray."

Fire thawed
icicles back into
fingers.

Orla

I was interviewed twice. The second time for them to tell me Zig had given in under questioning. When I came out of the interview room I ended up face to face with 'Taz' (Toby, apparently) – the creep with the roaming eyes from the Bothy. But sitting between two police officers, all curled in on himself, he didn't look too clever. He peered up at me as I passed, and I felt like having a real go at him. But then I caught the sparks of fear in his eyes. I wanted to hate him but he looked so alone, I couldn't. I never imagined I'd give him another thought after what they did to you, he deserves to be punished, but I still can't help wondering how he got to be like that. Why was no one there for him?

With his confession all the missing pieces fitted into place, except for you … still out there somewhere, maybe even concussed in the snow.

I dreaded going back to Greenlands. It didn't even look like home. I got out of the car, willing one thing to have been saved, holding my breath, desperately hoping it had not been destroyed by the flames… Most of the old trees were charred but there stood Sula's tree, her delicate branches covered in snow, and above the raven you called Bow sat as lookout, guarding it. Whenever I saw Bow I felt so sad that, wherever you were, your raven had not gone with you.

The police got me to walk round the flat to see if I could spot anything missing. The raven coffin-box was gone – I'd guessed that already – and I hunted around for the the leaf from Sula's tree I'd placed in your hand. Didn't seem much point in telling anyone about that leaf but I hoped you were carrying it with you. Janice thought maybe you'd gone off to try to see your dad, but every day the police checked but no one called at the hospital.

At first when they brought Taz in he tried to lay the blame for the fire and the stolen bikes on you and Zig. He made out that it was you two who planned it all because you had the keys to the Bothy. They found traces of petrol in your flat and in the Bothy too, but Zig had already put them right.

The cordons were removed. Now there was a clear path through from Greenlands, past where the Bothy used to be, to the Rec. A clear track through but everyone walked round the roads, and the Bothy became a great guilt-charred hole in the centre of our world.

The smell of destruction lingered long after the Bothy, the site of all our growing up, was cleared. Above it the blackened trees were covered thicker every day with fresh, clean snow. The untouched silvery branches of Sula's tree and the raven that would not leave were our Greenlands Guardians now.

Bow seemed to be waiting there for you, looking out over the eye-shaped patch of ash.

I couldn't answer Zak's texts and constant calls so instead I walked down to Sula's tree and placed my arms round her trunk and cried and cried and cried for you to come home.

Yannis kept coming back to see if I could give them any more details of how you were that last time I saw you. They fused my description together with the last school photograph Janice had given them. A boy with a halo of curls and soft round cheeks.

But the photofit looked nothing like you. I knew why… Neither of those people were really you. I couldn't even give them a description of what you were wearing because you got yourself dressed while I was asleep and not in the bloodstained clothes I found you in. The police said the most likely way of identifying you was through the bike, the tattoos and your injured hand. Zak's dad gave them a picture of the model and make. I thought it was sad that they were more likely to identify you through a stolen bike than your face.

A few days after the fire I read a report in the paper Mum brought home. I'd seen these posters before at bus stops and on Tube stations.

MISSING AFTER RAVENSCROFT FIRE

Sixteen-year-old local boy Kai King went missing on the night of the fire at Ravenscroft Rec. He was riding a new silver Ridgeback bike. His left hand is injured and may be broken. After initial fears that he had been caught up in the blaze police are now searching for his whereabouts. There is reason to believe that Kai may need mental health support. His name has now been placed on a register of vulnerable missing persons. If anyone has any further information about this enquiry please contact:

As I read the missing person poster over and over I had this thought, one that should be obvious to me before. That every story of a person missing or lost was not just news, but someone who is loved like you.

The poster haunted me, especially as I'd overheard Yannis say, "My worry is he's just at that cusp age when sometimes young homeless kids slip through the net. It won't help that he looks older and all roughed up."

"What net?" I wanted to scream. It made me sick to think of you roaming about in the freezing snow and even sicker when everyone kept going on about how beautiful the snow was. All I could think of was you somewhere out there on the streets, desperately trying to keep warm, afraid to come home to face the mess you'd left behind.

Then came Advent and the counting of the days. Mum bought me the usual chocolate calendar but I didn't really have the heart to open it.

Watching ice breath,
I thought he was my friend,
shared food with me.
But when I slept
he stole my wings.
I sang and sang
a song I remembered.
A song of bleak midwinter.

One time, looking over the Rec for you as I did every day, I saw that old man – do you remember him? The one who said he built the Bothy, who came with his daughter and his dog when we were kids. I felt a bit guilty because over the years I haven't even thought of him. Anyway, the woman must have been pretty determined to get the old man out and about because she'd pushed him through the snow in a wheelchair, a big blanket over his knees. They were right there in the place our Bothy used to be.

The old man's arms were raised above his head and he looked like he was making a huge effort to tell the woman something as he pointed in a wide arc from Sula's tree to the school buildings. He seemed agitated and I felt like running down to them and telling the woman that what he said was true – there was a Bothy here and once upon a time it had been a happy place for us. One we would never have discovered without him.

There were so many 'should have dones' at that time, Kai. I just stood there as the woman pushed the old man, slowly wheeling through the snow. I stayed there for ages, watching them become smaller and smaller and wondering if one day everything that we'd been to each other would fade to nothing too. I cried a lot that day, Kai.

For you, for the old man, for all the happy memories of building our little Bothy.

I began to think that with you a piece of us all had slipped away, that my own grip on reality was failing. It was as if we were all snow-blind.

I didn't go into school that day. I just felt too sad, remembering how sweet life had been when we were all huddled in the den. It was 5th December and I opened the window on the calendar and ate the chocolate. I looked at all the unopened Advent windows and thought I can't just let the days go by and do nothing.

I felt like
when I buried Rain
I took on all his pain.
I saw the world
through his broken eye.

I became obsessed with standing on my balcony and watching out for signs of your return. I used to love snow, but now every morning it grew deeper, it seemed intent on covering over every trace of you. A white wall of silence. Even I could see that it made Greenlands look beautiful again, like the fire had never been, wiping out our past.

Frankie was out every day with a group of volunteers, searching for you, posting leaflets through doors. Zak, Om and I went out with him a few times after school but it felt hopeless and after a while I couldn't bring myself to.

You'd been gone a whole week when Faith contacted me to ask if I was coming to the next Greenlands Guardians meeting. I knew we should fight on even harder now for your sake, but I just couldn't. I couldn't sleep, I couldn't eat. Faith must have called my mum and without asking a single question Mum offered to go in my place.

Since you had left she'd kind of got her mettle up and, even though your mum rejected her at first, she came to trust that my mum was there for her. Mum persuaded Janice to join the Greenlands Guardians and it gave her something to focus on. I watched them go, your mum and mine, linking arms together, marching across the Rec with Om and his Aunt Gisou. Their footprints marked their path in the snow and I was so proud of Mum for rallying and fighting to keep things together, when I could not.

Looking at their footprints, I thought, *I was wrong not to involve Mum before.*

You say you lost your words, Kai, well, I think I did too for a while.

December days stumbled on, growing colder, snow falling and freezing, falling and freezing. Every hour that there was no news of you I grew more numb inside. Nothing really touched me. Not even the stress I would usually feel about exams... In fact having to sit down to revise for hour after hour was a welcome place of retreat instead of thinking of you and where you were during what everyone said was "the coldest winter in a century".

Zak and me and Om would get together sometimes, mostly to see if there was any news. Zak said his dad's bike had been found with a homeless man who claimed it was abandoned. Joel said he would have given anything for you to have come home instead. The police were going to put out the missing photo again, that's all he knew.

I was no one, nothing more than a shadow-Kai.
Silent as snow, drifting across that bridge.

Then Om called it. "With that image of the tough boy with frozen eyes they will never find him." He was sure of it.

It was his idea for me to describe exactly how you looked the night you left. He said he knew your face better than anyone, the expression in your eyes. And what he drew looked so like you the night you held the beheaded raven, it nearly broke my heart.

Yannis made sure that Om's drawing went into the newspapers. I saw it in bus stops and on the Tube when Zak, Om and I spent our weekends aimlessly looking for you. Somehow any tension there had been between me and Zak just drifted away because all we ever thought about was you. We never spoke about it, but as we trudged through the snow we were thinking that our childhood pact to always stick together was coming true, but only because you were missing. We all wished the same thing… That we had not left it too late.

Om's new portrait of you gave us a bit of hope. We walked all over the place, handing out flyers, but no one had seen you.

I reckon that at first not a single student or teacher walked into the Rec without a thought for you, Kai, but it seemed that as the days passed people spoke of you less.

And, as Christmas holidays approached, all the brightly dressed, bobble-hatted children from primary filled the Rec with their joy and snowball fights. It looked like a perfect picture-book Christmas holiday scene, but for us the shadow of your absence hung over everything.

Every morning your lonely raven would perch on my balcony, as if I needed reminding that you were gone. I wished it wouldn't.

I refused all Faith's offers of going to see that therapist at school, you know, the one she wanted you to go to as well. Me getting help when you were out there on your own just felt wrong. If I wasn't working my mind went to the night I found you, over and over and over again replaying it in my mind... What I should have, could have done.

In any case, the only person who seemed to understand was Om. I got then what he had tried to do for you.

"Orla, you must find a way to survive now, through this pain… Maybe you can paint too?"

I tried to make light of it. "Have you seen my art, Om?"

But he was serious. "Then run – place your footsteps in the snow, one after the other, and feel where you are in this moment."

I hugged him then for his kindness. "Thought I was supposed to be *your* mentor!"

And after that I did start to run again.

Omid

Since the fire and the Greenlands Guardians meetings Aunt Gisou had started to be more familiar with people in the tower. Your mother and Orla's mother became closer friends and invited Aunt Gisou to eat with them, so she returned the invitation. I was so happy but sad also that now we were in this community, without my brothers. I wondered how many brothers I could lose? For the first time my aunt was more settled than me.

It was Aunt Gisou's idea to plant the Christmas rose beside the Sula tree. She did not believe that any flower could survive this snow, so when she discovered it in the garden centre she said she felt hope in her heart for Kai and Ishy too.

I remembered then how she used to scatter seeds on our long journey here to lift my spirits, planting new orchards on our way.

She told me, "When this boy comes home he will know that we have planted good wishes for him, here on this land we have flown to."

At the planting of the winter rose Aunt Gisou brought a candle. Orla invited Zak but she would not allow anyone else to dig in this place and would not let me or Zak help her.

So it was that Orla found the box containing the dead raven. I finally understood that is what I saw you do that day standing by the Sula tree, burying the bird … and then we also knew why the living raven now guards this land, through loyalty.

Tears came from all our eyes and lungs and hearts for you, Kai. For once the living raven grew still and silent as Orla respectfully planted the rose above the raven grave and secured it in the cold, cold earth. Behind us, I saw how your mother held hands with Aunt Gisou and quietly my aunt began to speak her memories of vigils on the road for those who were left behind.

The women held each other in a desperate embrace. I saw Orla grasp Zak's hand and then he took a tube from his bag. He and Orla placed it in some liquid and blew one giant bubble from where they were standing by the tree. I did not understand their meaning but your mother broke down and Orla's mother hugged her. Zak placed his hand on my shoulder and explained to me that you used to do this as children, and asked for me to make a wish too.

I wished that you, my brothers Kai and Ishy, could return to me. I wished that Kai's father would come home. We did not talk but only watched the giant bubble float across Greenlands, catching rainbow light and changing shape when floating for a long, long time before it met snow-earth and melted.

Orla

Planting that rose and blowing the bubble shifted something I thought was dead in me ... the will to fight for our little patch of wilderness with or without the Bothy. I looked down over the snow-covered Rec where no borders or boundaries existed as far as anyone could see. It had nothing to do with what side of the Rec we lived on. Nothing to do with owning it for ourselves. We already do because, no matter what a piece of paper says, this tiny bit of earth is our land. The land of our childhood and if it belongs to anyone it belongs to us.

I got it in my head that day that keeping Greenlands safe and you coming home were bound together and if we stopped fighting for our bit of turf then we would be giving up on you too.

Zak said to tell you his wish has never changed.

So anyway I got my mettle up like Mum and started speaking out at the meetings again.

I grew so tired of battling, Om.

Omid

At first my thinking was like this. You are a strong boy. You will come home. I thought maybe at this time you need to be alone, but after two weeks had passed I was no longer sure. Every day that you were missing I placed myself further in my art.

These are the paintings I did in that waiting time. One, a Christmas rose beside the Sula tree as a gift for you when you return. A portrait of you, Kai, not weakened but strong, and something else... One small fig tree to show that, even after all this time, I do not give up hope to see you and my brother Ishy again.

Zak's mother thinks they are my best work and I must submit them for my GCSE exam pieces. I told her I have one more in this series I want to paint.

I stood where we stood ... before.
Planning, picturing, promising ourselves next trip to go inside.

I place my paintbrush on the paper. I plant trees and flowers and wish for Greenlands. I move away from fire. I know I must stay in the light for my aunt and I must stay in the light for my brothers too.

These are the words I used to *annotate* my art.

When she read my words Orla smiled at me, as if she was saying, "And what about me?", so I added *also for my sister too.* Then we cried together, thinking of you.

Orla

On 18th December, the last day of school, I opened the Advent calendar for the second time. The chocolate was a little bear so I took it down to Sula's tree and laid it there beside the Christmas rose. Everything was a trigger.

People thought I organized the vigil, but actually it came together through communal will. We all had a part in it. Maybe everyone was looking for something to light your way.

Faith helped to rally the school too and you know how it is on the last day of term, especially with the Rec as it was then. A winter wonderland. Everyone stayed. The message for people to bring a candle for Kai spread far and wide, beyond anything we could have imagined. I could not believe how many gathered on the Rec, holding a candle for you and for Greenlands.

Below us were people I knew but so many I had never seen before. There were small children from the primary school, still wearing their outfits from the Christmas play, faces painted, standing with their families.

A group of nursery children with angel wings sticking out of their coats huddled together. At the back of the crowd I was surprised to see the boy Zig and his dad, though they kept their heads bowed.

Faith, my mum and Om's Aunt Gisou stayed close by my side and a little way back, where our den used to be, Zak's dad held Hope's hand, a silver halo on her head. But Janice was missing. If nothing else we thought this show of support might help her. I didn't want to speak until she was there, but there was this hush that happens when a crowd gathers, when you know it's time for something to begin. But how could we start without your mum?

Slowly moving along the bottom road I saw Frankie's car. Headlights flashing over and over and your mum got out and then … your dad climbed out, holding your mum's arm. They walked slowly up the hill to stand together by Sula's tree. Frankie slipped away into the crowd.

Your dad looked taller than I remembered and so thin. Like he'd been through a storm. "Hello, Orlie." My heart ached for both of them as I handed your mum the candle, struck a match and lit it, just as we arranged. She turned to your dad and placed it in his hands.

Turning to all the people gathered there, he took in one deep breath, and loud and clear he blasted these words over the Rec – "For Kai and Greenlands." And all the voices echoed back as he placed the candle by Sula's tree.

"Orlie, hug!" Hope broke free of Joel and came running up the hill to me.

I watched her determined little face and cringed inside as Joel tried to stop her. I wished he would stop calling her name but your dad smiled. "Let Hope come," he whispered.

I picked her up and all the time, above us, the raven you'd named Bow called, "Kai, Kai, Kai." I thought my heart would shatter.

Om had pictured how things should run. So one by one he invited people to step forward and place their candles on the white carpet of snow that covered the Bothy ground.

The woman with the dog went first, the old man no longer her side. She lit her candle and placed it where the Bothy had been. I wanted to ask her where the old man was, if he was OK, but I lost her in the crowd.

After all the candles had been placed the Bothy was transformed into the shape Om had marked out in the snow – a giant shining eye.

"All this light and hope for my Kai must bring him home," your dad whispered, wiping away his tears. I saw how your mum and dad looked at each other with such love and I wished that you would walk back into the Rec right at this moment to see it and feel all this love.

There we stood until the flames began to fade and slowly everyone left, except for your parents who stood beside Sula's tree long after the last candle burned out.

And over the following days I saw strangers light a candle for Kai while they watched their children play in the snow and I thought what Om's Aunt Gisou said to him was true. "The bright eye of hope will not be easily forgotten in this community."

Look to the shine in their eye, Kai.
"What do you want of us? For what
do you search?" the ravens cried.

Look to the shine
in their eye, Kai.
Inside I saw my reflection
lit against the snow.

"I wish to set us free, to fly inside. I wish to sing."
"Then come!" they cawed and flew me to where the songbirds sing.

Om, my brother,
I remember you.
Listening to the bleak midwinter choir,
this candle I light is for you and your brother Ishy,
and Sula, Sula, Sula...
The scent of light on silver leaf
draws me home.

'In the Bleak Midwinter.'
How did it even go?
That song Dad used to play.
These legs, heavy as stones,
trudging through snow.
First steps, Kai.
First steps.

Kai

It takes me until Easter to get back into school. Even though I'll have to wait a year to take my GCSEs, Faith's got my back. Taken me under her wing. I won't lie: it was humiliating being so behind but I have other things on my mind. Dad and me are taking the lead on the Greenlands Guardians campaign.

At school Faith tries to keep me occupied and she asks me to consult with the staff welfare team over how to help the kids who might be struggling. When we got back after the summer, I started mentoring a boy called Sunil and a girl called Leena. And after a while I seem to get through to them. It makes me feel less like a hanger-on – still taking my GCSEs when all my mates are have moved on to A-levels.

Hilarious that Sunil thinks I'm an actual teacher. Sometimes he forgets I'm Kai and calls me "Sir"! Faith goes on about me having a gift and keeps asking if I've ever thought of teaching. I think she must be joking but she seems serious enough.

I tell her connecting with them isn't exactly rocket science and she laughs. "Trust me, Kai. Sometimes it feels like it!"

Two years on, still one to go for me. I invite Sunil and Leena along to Om's final A-level exhibition, not expecting either of them to show but Sunil does! I keep it low key, not pushing it, but Dad takes Sunil straight under his wing. Something about us being together makes me look at Sunil and see myself not that long ago. I realize that Faith was right after all... Working with Sunil and Leena really has been the start of something.

Om's nervous. I can tell that when he welcomes us to "The Bothy". I can't believe he's achieved all this.

As we walk in we read together the words written on the wall. "This exhibition is dedicated to my brothers and sisters found and lost."

"Bit deep!" Sunil looks up at me but stops in his tracks when I tell him to have some respect.

Om's moved on so much from what he used to paint. Even from here, I can see that this is art to raise us up, out of reality. The charcoal lines are there but I notice soft colours too. I've never seen Om use colour like this before. I wander around in a daze, staring at his art that flies us way beyond our little low heaven.

"All right, mate?" Zak has seen I'm overwhelmed, says

he'll keep an eye on Sunil but he doesn't need to – Sunil's spellbound too.

His face makes me break into a smile because he's wide-eyed and still for a change. He's supposed to have problems concentrating but he can, if it's something that he wants to understand.

"Is Om like Banksy or something, Sir?" Sunil asks, staring at a painting that's half boy, half raven, dancing over flames. "This is you, isn't it? In these paintings? What does it mean?"

"You'll have to ask Om but I think this one's kind of saying something like … every single one of us deserves to fly!"

Sunil squirms away from me and I laugh out loud at the look on his face. It's the same sneer I used give Faith when she would praise me.

"He's doing well!" Orla smiles, tucking her hair behind her ear, and just then I catch sight of a tiny butterfly tattoo on her wrist.

"When did you get that? I didn't think you were into tattoos!"

"Well, I wasn't but I am now! Got it at the weekend."

"What does it mean?"

She grins. "I dunno, Kai! Just something we did for a laugh, Chidi and me. Didn't think too much about it!

We're not all Om – it doesn't have to mean anything."

I nod but press my palm against hers and just then sunshine blasts into the studio, dazzling us all.

"Are you two going out with each other, Sir?" Sunil interrupts us, sparks of mischief flying from his eyes.

"No, we are not," I say loud and clear, and for the first time that fact doesn't break my heart.

After Om's exhibition we run out of Ravenscroft, getting soaked in a sudden shower of summer rain. Me, Orla, Zak and Om ... and it feels like we're kids again. Not caring how muddy or soaked through we get. Orla's laughter lights up Greenlands as she challenges me to a sprint up our hill. We're sliding all over the place! It's close and we're side by side when she throws out her arms to make me stop because there in front of us is Bow, lying at the foot of Sula's tree.

And as we bury Bow beside her Rain, I can't throw off the feeling that Bow stood by till I was ready to fly.

When I eventually look up from writing the sun's chasing its last shadows over the Rec. I clear out the wilting flowers left for Bow and I know it's time to let her and all the other shadows go.

This has probably been the hardest thing I've ever had to do – writing this, like trying to cut through the wilderness of my own mind that tangles as fast as I clear it.

My fingers trace along the last torn pages of this notebook's spine; the jagged edges of all my rejected endings – what could have been, and what was.

Epilogue

I'm packing away Om's portfolio when my phone pings. I check my screen...

Here we are, just hours ago. Caught in time forever by Sula's tree. Me, Orla, Om and Zak.

I can't believe that was only this morning. Reading my way through our past has made present time slow. I pack away Om's portfolio.

In the distance I watch as one by one the lights of Ravenscroft sixth-form block are switched off. *Is that Faith?* I wonder, then remember the letter that Zak gave me. I pull it out of my pocket. The envelope isn't addressed to me personally.

To the Greenlands Guardians campaign

The letter has already been opened. It's probably one of Faith's projects to keep me focused I think as I take out the letter.

I am writing following the death of my father. He told me several times that he built a Bothy on the site of Greenlands.

I rock on my heels and settle back down to read. The sharp bark of an old man's dog rewinds in my mind to what feels like ancient times … or a fairy tale when three little faces peeped through the slates of a den

My father suffered from dementia and towards the end of his life came to stay with me. We were unaware that he had ever lived in London before, but it has come to light that he had difficult teenage years that he never spoke of and did in fact live here for a while. Soon after he moved in with us he seemed drawn to Greenlands, although he could not explain why, so I would sometimes take him there.

We have recently discovered that when he was just fourteen years old he worked as a gardener for Ravenscroft House, that later became the school. He built his own bothy there as a little hideaway and perhaps a memory of happy childhood days in the Highlands.

It's taken me a while to sort out my father's possessions. He was a self-educated man and had many books. I was intrigued to find one about Highland bothies and I was

looking through it when I came across this map. It shows that the land the bothy was built on actually belonged to the school, but the land you call the 'Greenlands wood' and the adjacent Rec is named here as 'Ancient Common Land'.

I read about the Greenlands Guardians campaign to save the Rec from development in the news. The day my father passed away I joined a vigil on the Rec. I found myself lighting a candle for my father, as well as for the missing boy. Afterwards I was happy to hear of his return, like Dad had been with me somehow.

It turned out, in a way, that he was. I'm not sure if the map my father drew can be of any use to you and your campaign. Sadly we can no longer recover this lost chapter of my father's life, but it felt right to hand this over. I hope it can be of value to your campaign...

My fingers tremble as I place the letter that feels like it's fallen out of the sky back in its envelope. I take my pen back out of my pocket, tuck the envelope into the final page of my notebook and turn is over to write the new beginning. As I do I'm blasted by the bright, sweet voice of a song thrush. I close my eyes, picturing the words that flow now from my pen as they sing through me.

Dedicated to
Dad, Mum, Sula,
Omid, Orla Zak,
Faith, Rain and Bow
and an old man
whose name I don't even know.
You are the gold at the end of this rainbow.

Acknowledgments

When Shadows Fall could not have been written without the inspiration, passion and support of many people in my life spanning back to the beginning of work in community and youth theatre. There is not space here to thank them all but if our paths have crossed on the writing, art or theatre way and we have worked together or spent time discussing how best to access and help young people find freedom of expression then please accept my sincere thanks.

The confidence to publish my writing did not come till I had a family of my own. My first thanks to my great love Leo and our three amazing grown up children Maya, Keshin and Esha who, together, are the greatest inspirations and encouragement in life and writing.

Huge thanks to Sophie Gorell Barnes of MBA Literary Agents who has always had faith in this novel and seen it through many incarnations till it found its place at Little Tiger, commissioned by Ruth Bennett. From the start I worked with both Ruth and my editor Mattie Whitehead on this story. Both of their deep insights, nurturing and encouragement have made this book what it is today. Mattie's belief in this novel and dedication and talent to see this story home through the trials of lockdown, including an editorial in the Rec that inspired the location, is something I'll never forget.

I would like to thank all the incredible team at Little Tiger and everyone else who worked on the book so that they are seen and celebrated for their deep passion for this story and care in publishing it. Ruth Bennett, Mattie Whitehead, Charlie Moyler, Lauren Ace, Nina Douglas, Dannie Price, Summer Lanchester, George Hanratty, Sarah Shaffi, Kate Newcombe, Demet Hoffmeyer, Nicola O'Connell, Tom Truong, Lucy Rogers and Jane Tait.

It is especially moving to me that Lauren Ace was there at the beginning of my writing journey when I was writing the first drafts of this novel and that Lauren has become such a wonderful author herself.

The illustrator of this book Natalie Sirett has been a friend since our own children were in nursery. Easels in the garden and sari tents were part of our own parenting iconography. I have admired Natalie's incredible storytelling in art since then. I gave Natalie a draft of this story many years ago and was overwhelmed by the imagery she presented me with in response. I cannot thank Natalie enough for the inspiration she brings to this novel or to Charlie Moyler for her incredible work together on the Design – for what cannot be expressed in words by these young characters is held in art.

Thank you to the incredible community of Islington Centre for Refugees and Migrants especially to wonderful friends Jane Ray and Ros Asquith and all the people who have attended the class over the years and felt the healing powers of art and writing.

My own dedication is to Robby Sukhdeo whom I first met when we moved into our home twenty years ago. I am in awe of the way he has transformed a piece of neglected urban land with the help of his family and community and worked with such faith and imagination and care for all the young people who found their way there. I have watched year by year as the Rec, now Oliver Tambo Recreation Ground, has become a fittingly named walkway to freedom, play, education, leisure time, equality, potential and community cohesion. Robbie's patience and guidance has changed the lives of many young people and their hopes, histories, losses and laughter all planted on that Rec. As for the ravens... I've watched their ways for many years too, and have them to thank for Rain and Bow.

Thanks to wonderful authors Az Dassu, Gill Lewis, Nicola Penfold and Jasbinder Bilan for their encouragement in reading early copies of this story and to for the insights and advice of Sarah Shaffi. Thanks to Onjali Q Rauf, Maya Sanbar and Juliet Stevenson, Nicky Parker and the team at Amnesty International for being daily inspirations to follow paths of communal light over shadows.

My deepest thanks go to the many young people I have worked with and mentored over a thirty year career in the arts, youth theatre, education and writing, for all that you have taught and teach me; threads and wishes of lightful journeys forward are marked into these pages. Last and most heartfelt thanks go to you, readers for picking up this book... I hope you find your own way to express what cannot always be held in one linear form.

Author's Note

What a life's journey it's been writing *When Shadows Fall*. The young characters began emerging many years ago and the layers of this story peel back to my beginnings in community with young people, exploding with potential but already excluded from school. From them I learned what happens when the safety nets of family and societal support and the long term impacts of racism fail young people.

I have worked in Art Education for the last thirty years, helping develop the potential of vulnerable young people in society, offering the arts as a way through the tempests they face. This story is an homage to the young who are walking this earth in the shadows, and in them you will find people of great courage and agency, striving to fulfil their dreams and crying out to be helped.

Refugee survivor people have always been central to this work. I have found inspiration in art as well as writing as a means of expressing what may not be easy to speak. From this potential-freeing work Omid was born. I always knew that his art would be key to the telling of this story. It is a matter of great creative fulfilment to me to pass the words that cannot be spoken to Natalie Sirett to find their expression in art. Our symbolic worlds need nurturing all our lives and we lose the illustrations from novels just when we need them most. I am so happy that they are central to this story.

Time and again I have seen how the experience of finding a voice through drama, writing, dance, singing, art, painting, playing and access to nature has been the saving grace of many young people. These are the most undervalued and invisible safety nets of creativity.

In the years since these characters came to me the number of exclusions from school has risen to shocking numbers and the crisis in mental health is now impacting the majority of families and communities. During the global COVID pandemic all children have experienced what it is like to be on the outside of the school gates.

If you or your friends are struggling with mental health concerns, don't hesitate to reach out. There's no stigma in seeking help. Tell a family member, friend, a trusted person in your school, college or university or your GP. If it would be easier to speak to someone outside of your community there are charities that exist to help, including Young Minds and Papyrus, a suicide prevention charity. You can find their contacts online.

I'm a believer that stories wait for their time. *When Shadows Fall* is published into times where globally and in the UK we have never seen greater inequality between the most resourced and poorest in society. Access to education has been everyone's business but it is the most vulnerable who will have the highest hill to climb. It seems fitting to me that Kai and his friends, who have faced the trauma and survived, tell this tale from the top of their green hill sending out a message of resilience and hope.

I hope this novel will be a catalyst for many new writers and artists seeking what is truly golden to be discovered at the end of the rainbow. With great hope for the future, I pass this pen.

About the Author

Sita Brahmachari is a writer of critically acclaimed, widely read novels, novellas, short stories and plays. She has a background in working in youth and community theatre and has an MA in Arts Education. She won the Waterstones Children's Book Prize with her debut novel Artichoke Hearts and her writing of Tender Earth was honoured by the International Board of Books for Young People. Her many novels have been shortlisted for the UKLA Book Award, The Little Rebel Award, nominated for the CILIP Carnegie Medal, and have been translated into many languages around the world. She was The Booktrust Writer in Residence and is the Writer in Residence at Islington Centre for Refugees and Migrants. Sita is an Amnesty International ambassador and a Royal Literary Fellow. She lives in London with her family.

About the Illustrator

Natalie Sirett is an internationally exhibited, multimedia artist, interested in us, our icons, our stories. Her work has often explored issues of body image culture and the growing pains of adolescence. *When Shadows Fall* is a project shared with Sita Brahmachari over many years and she is delighted that it has come to fruition. Natalie lives and works in London.